Jessica's in big trouble . . .

"Jessica Wakefield," Lila screamed. "I can't believe you would do something like this! And you're supposed to be my friend!"

Jessica shook her head, looking confused. "Lila, I told you I was sorry about what happened in homeroom, but I don't see why you have to have a conniption fit over it—"

"I'll show you what happened in homeroom," Lila cried, so loudly that students in the hallway stopped and turned to see what was happening.

Lila lunged toward Jessica's locker, pushing Jessica out of the way. "What happened in homeroom is that you stole my Watchman!"

"Lila, you must be kidding!" Jessica protested. "Have you lost your mind?"

"No," Lila yelled, "but you've definitely lost a friend!" She reached into the messy top shelf of Jessica's locker and fished around. Suddenly she withdrew her hand and held something up for everyone to see. "My Watchman!" she cried triumphantly.

"But . . ." Jessica's voice trailed off. "But . . . Lila, I-I didn't take it! I have no idea how it got there!"

Bantam Skylark Books in the SWEET VALLEY TWINS AND FRIENDS series.
Ask your bookseller for the books you have missed.

Sweet Valley Twins and Friends Super Editions

Sweet Valley Twins and Friends Super Chiller Editions

Sweet Valley Twins and Friends Magna Edition

SWEET VALLEY TWINS AND FRIENDS®

Jessica the Thief

Written by
Jamie Suzanne

Created by
FRANCINE PASCAL

A BANTAM SKYLARK BOOK
NEW YORK · TORONTO · LONDON · SYDNEY · AUCKLAND

RL 4, 008–012

JESSICA THE THIEF
A Bantam Skylark Book / March 1993

Sweet Valley High® and Sweet Valley Twins and Friends®
are registered trademarks of Francine Pascal

Conceived by Francine Pascal

Produced by Daniel Weiss Associates, Inc.
33 West 17th Street
New York, NY 10011

Cover art by James Mathewuse

Skylark Books is a registered trademark of Bantam Books, a division
of Bantam Doubleday Dell Publishing Group, Inc. Registered in U.S.
Patent and Trademark Office and elsewhere.

ISBN 0-553-48054-5

Published simultaneously in the United States and Canada

Bantam Books are published by Bantam Books, a division of Bantam
Doubleday Dell Publishing Group, Inc. Its trademark, consisting of
the words "Bantam Books" and the portrayal of a rooster, is Registered
in U.S. Patent and Trademark Office and in other countries. Marca
Registrada. Bantam Books, 666 Fifth Avenue, New York, New York
10103.

PRINTED IN THE UNITED STATES OF AMERICA
OPM   0 9 8 7 6 5 4 3 2 1

Jessica the Thief

One

◇

"Jessica, did you steal my new turquoise sweater?" Elizabeth Wakefield demanded, storming into her twin sister's bedroom on Sunday night.

Jessica Wakefield looked up from the magazine she was reading. She recognized the look on her twin's face. Elizabeth was in a bad mood. A *very* bad mood.

"Steal?" Jessica echoed innocently. "*Steal* is such an ugly word, Lizzie. I prefer *borrow*."

Elizabeth put her hands on her hips and glared at her sister. "If you *borrowed* my sweater, why hasn't it been returned?"

Jessica scanned her pink-carpeted floor, which was covered with a thick layer of clothes and magazines. "Trust me, Elizabeth," she said with a shrug. "You don't want to wear that sweater. The wool is itchy. And besides, it really isn't a good color for you."

"If a color doesn't look good on me, why would it look good on you?"

Jessica rolled her eyes. She hated it when her twin used logic to win an argument. But she knew that Elizabeth was right. Physically, the girls were identical. They each had long, blond hair and blue-green eyes. They wore the same size clothes, and each girl had a dimple in her left cheek.

But in a lot of ways, the twins were very different. Jessica spent all her free time with the other members of the Unicorn Club, a group of the prettiest, most popular girls at Sweet Valley Middle School. The Unicorns held meetings once a week to discuss topics such as boys, rock stars, clothes, and makeup tips.

Elizabeth had attended a Unicorn meeting once and had almost dozed off. She preferred to spend her spare time working on the sixth-grade newspaper, *The Sweet Valley Sixers*, or reading a good mystery novel. She also enjoyed hanging out with her good friends Amy Sutton, Julie Porter, and Maria Slater, or with her sort-of boyfriend, Todd Wilkins.

"You're still not answering my question," Elizabeth said. "Where's my sweater?"

"I'm sure it's around here someplace," Jessica

said vaguely. She began digging through a huge mountain of dirty clothes at the foot of her bed. "Give me just a minute—"

"I could give you a year and you'd still be digging through that pile," Elizabeth said with a wry smile. "You know, I don't really mind if you want to wear my clothes. But the least you could do is *ask* before you take them."

"I *did* ask," Jessica said. "Remember? You were on the phone with Amy."

"I don't remember that. What did I say?"

Jessica reached deeper into the pile. "Hey, would you settle for these socks I borrowed last week? I only wore them once."

"Jessica," Elizabeth said. "What did I say when you asked if you could borrow my sweater?"

"You didn't exactly *say* anything," Jessica replied. "But you sort of nodded."

Elizabeth sighed. "A sort-of nod isn't exactly a definite yes, Jessica. This isn't the first time something you've 'borrowed' of mine has disappeared, by the way."

"Name three things!" Jessica cried indignantly.

"My silver bracelet, my denim skirt, and my white blouse," Elizabeth said, ticking the items off on her fingers.

Jessica sighed. "I promise, cross my heart, that your sweater is here . . . somewhere." She peered under her mattress hopefully, but Elizabeth was already walking out the door. "Elizabeth," Jessica called. "Don't you believe me?"

Elizabeth looked over her shoulder. "Just promise me this is the last thing you steal, okay?"

"I promise not to steal anything else," Jessica replied with a grin. "But do you think maybe I could *borrow* your new yellow miniskirt to wear to school tomorrow?"

"I love your skirt, Jessica," Veronica Brooks said as she fell into step beside Jessica and Elizabeth. It was Monday, and the twins were walking down the hall together toward the lunchroom.

"Thanks," Jessica and Elizabeth both answered at the same time. They quickly glanced at each other, and Jessica raised an eyebrow.

Just a few weeks earlier, Veronica had tried to steal Todd Wilkins away from Elizabeth at a school dance. She also had been openly mean and nasty to both Elizabeth and Jessica when they spoiled her plans. She had even threatened Jessica with revenge at one point. But a few days later, Veronica had apologized to both twins, and had gone so far out of her way to be nice to them that they'd stopped being quite so mad at her.

Veronica smiled. "So do you guys share your clothes a lot?" she asked.

"Sometimes," Jessica replied.

"Whether we want to or not," Elizabeth added.

"Well, you always look so great," Veronica said to Jessica, her voice filled with admiration. "I wish I had such wonderful taste." The girls paused in front of the lunchroom door. "Well," Veronica said. "I have to go get my lunch, but I guess I'll be seeing you at the Unicorner, Jessica."

"You're eating with us?" Jessica asked in surprise. Usually the table where the Unicorns ate lunch each day, which they had nicknamed the Unicorner, was strictly for members only.

"I hope it's OK," Veronica said. "Lila invited me. I'm so excited. I mean, who wouldn't be? It's a pretty big honor."

Jessica tossed her head and smiled proudly. "True."

"I'll see you in a few minutes," Veronica said as she hurried off down the hall.

"Since when is Veronica a friend of Lila Fowler's?" Elizabeth asked when Veronica was out of earshot.

"Well, they are neighbors," Jessica pointed out. "And lately Veronica's been hanging around the Unicorns a lot."

"I wonder why?"

"Why?" Jessica repeated. "Isn't it obvious why? We're only the most important, popular girls in school, Elizabeth."

"How could I forget?" Elizabeth said with a

grin. "I must have gone into temporary brain-lock."

Jessica ignored her twin's teasing. "You know, Veronica has been incredibly nice lately, don't you think?" she asked as she watched Veronica turn the corner at the end of the hall.

"Yeah, she has."

"Especially to the Unicorns. I think she really wants to be friends with us."

Elizabeth frowned. "But after everything she did, do *you* want to be friends with *her?*"

Jessica shrugged. "She did apologize for all that. And she's certainly making up for it now. She's always asking us to come over, and having her housekeeper make us great food. She has an awesome house, and a huge pool. Janet thinks she's potential Unicorn material. She's pretty, she dresses well—"

"She's superficial," Elizabeth added. "Not to mention sneaky."

Jessica patted her twin on the shoulder. "I don't blame you if you're still mad about what happened at the dance, Lizzie. Trying to steal Todd was a really rotten thing for Veronica to do."

Elizabeth sighed. "Well, Veronica isn't exactly my best friend, but I'm not mad anymore. After all, Todd and I are fine now, and you and Aaron are friends again, and Veronica and Bruce Patman actually seem like a happy couple. So I guess all's well that ends well. It's just hard for me to believe that Veronica's really changed."

"Give her a chance," Jessica urged.

"I guess you're right," Elizabeth admitted. "Everybody deserves a second chance. Even Veronica."

"Besides," Jessica added with a laugh, "she can't be all bad. She loves your taste in skirts!"

By the time Jessica made her way through the hot-lunch line, Veronica was already at the Unicorner. She and several of the Unicorns were gathered around Lila.

"What's everybody looking at?" Jessica asked as she set down her tray.

"My new Watchman," Lila said. "Daddy gave it to me last night. He just got back from New York, and I made him promise to bring me something extra special."

Jessica couldn't help feeling a twinge of jealousy. Mr. Fowler was one of the richest people in Sweet Valley, and he bought Lila almost anything she wanted. "Let's see," Jessica said.

Lila passed the miniature TV to Jessica. "Just think," Lila said excitedly. "I can actually watch *Days of Turmoil* during class!"

Mandy Miller laughed. "That'll be the day. I'd like to see you try to watch soap operas during math class!"

"I've got to get one of these," Jessica said as

she passed the Watchman back to Lila. "Are they expensive?"

Lila nodded. "Outrageously."

Too bad, Jessica thought bleakly. The last time she had checked, she had had a grand total of one dollar and seventy-three cents in savings.

"You are *so* lucky to have such a cool dad, Lila," Veronica said.

"She's also lucky to have such a cool best friend," Jessica added as she opened her milk. She gave Lila a big smile. "The kind of best friend who can borrow anything she wants because Lila's so generous. Right, Lila?"

Lila scowled. "Dream on, Jessica. Like I'd ever let you borrow something this expensive."

"So much for her generosity," Belinda Layton said, laughing.

"I'm very generous," Lila cried indignantly. "Didn't I lend you my extra backpack the other day, Jessica?"

"You mean the one with the hole in the bottom?" Jessica said. "Halfway home, my social-studies homework fell out and landed in a puddle. I couldn't even read it."

"I'll bet Mrs. Arnette loved that excuse," Mandy Miller said.

"Anyway," Lila continued defensively, "I do lend you things, Jessica. But I could never trust you with something as expensive as my Watchman. You're not exactly reliable, you know."

"Me, unreliable?" Jessica demanded. She couldn't believe Lila would say that. It was bad enough to hear it from Elizabeth! "What are you talking about?"

"Well, there's that raspberry-banana lip gloss I let you borrow that you never returned. I didn't even get to try it."

"Um—" Ellen Riteman murmured. "That wasn't Jessica. That was me."

"See?" Jessica cried.

Lila spun around to face Ellen. "So where is it?"

"I'm not exactly sure," Ellen answered, staring at her plate. "It may be at my aunt's house in Newport Beach. Or else my mom washed it with a load of jeans last week. Or else—"

"Never mind." Lila threw up her hands. "I get the idea."

"I could buy you another one," Ellen offered.

"Just forget it," Lila said, pouting.

"If it makes you feel any better, it tasted like banana barf."

"Ellen, please," Janet Howell cried. "Some of us are trying to eat, you know."

"Sorry, Janet," Ellen said.

"*I'm* the one you should be apologizing to," Lila snapped.

"I didn't mean to lose your lip gloss," Ellen replied. "I guess I'm just forgetful. I'm always losing things."

"I know what you mean," Jessica said sympathetically.

"To tell you the truth, I was almost afraid to wear these earrings today," Ellen added. "They're my mom's, and if I lose them, she'll ground me until I'm eighteen."

"They're gorgeous," Jessica said. "Are they real silver?"

Ellen nodded. "They're also really heavy. I think I'll take them off for a few minutes. I feel like my earlobes are going to stretch to the floor." She removed the silver hoops and put them on the table.

"I'd love a pair of these," Jessica said as she picked up one of the earrings.

"They are beautiful," Veronica agreed.

"Do you know where your mom got them, Ellen?" Jessica asked.

"Mexico."

Jessica sighed as she put down the hoop. "I was hoping you'd say the mall."

Just then Mandy pointed toward the lunch line. "Good news, guys," she exclaimed. "Unless my cookie radar's wrong, they just put out a fresh batch of peanut-butter cookies!"

"Finally," Janet exclaimed, shoving back her chair. "Something I can eat without gagging."

"We'd better hurry," Mandy warned. "Those cookies usually go fast."

All of the Unicorns dashed for the lunch line.

Jessica and Veronica were the last to get in line, and by the time they got to the desserts, the only things left were fruit cups and brownies.

"Don't even think about eating one of those," Jessica warned as Veronica reached for a brownie. "That's a brownie brick. They're hard as rocks. Rumor has it those same three brownies have been here since the school opened twenty years ago."

Veronica laughed. "Jessica, you have such a great sense of humor."

Jessica couldn't help smiling. She was really beginning to like Veronica. "Well, I do crack myself up sometimes." She nodded toward the Unicorner. "Come on. Let's go see if they'll share some crumbs with us."

When Jessica and Veronica got back to the Unicorner, they found Ellen crawling on the floor under the table. "What's wrong, Ellen?" Jessica asked. "Looking for leftovers?"

"My mom's earrings!" Ellen cried frantically. "I can't find them anywhere!"

"Maybe someone stole them," Veronica suggested.

"That's crazy," Jessica said. "Nobody stole them."

"No?" Ellen said. "Then where are they?"

Jessica scanned the table. "They're bound to show up, Ellen," she said reassuringly. "Trust me. I lose stuff all the time, and it always turns up eventually. Well, almost always."

"What am I going to tell my mom?" Ellen moaned.

"Tell her you're irresponsible," Lila suggested. "And while you're at it, ask her if she's seen any lip gloss in the washing machine."

"This sure is weird," Mandy said. "I mean, where could the earrings have disappeared to? Maybe they really were stolen."

"There aren't any thieves at Sweet Valley Middle School," Jessica replied as she casually reached across the table toward Lila's lunch tray.

"Then how come half of my peanut-butter cookie just disappeared?" Lila demanded.

Jessica took a bite of cookie and smiled sweetly. "That's what I like about you, Lila," she said. "You're so incredibly generous."

Two

◇

When Jessica and Elizabeth got home from school that afternoon, they found their fourteen-year-old brother, Steven, in the kitchen with his friend Joe Howell, Janet's older brother. Both boys appeared to be working feverishly on their homework.

"Elizabeth," Jessica whispered loudly, grabbing her twin's arm. "I think there's something wrong with Steven." She circled the kitchen table slowly. "Look at the way his forehead's all scrunched up."

Elizabeth peered at her brother. "I've seen this look before," she said, trying not to smile. "About a year ago, I think it was."

Steven continued to concentrate on the paper in front of him.

"I'm going to go out on a limb here, Lizzie," Jessica whispered loudly. "I believe Steven may actually be *thinking!*"

"Do you mind?" Steven demanded. He consulted the timer on the kitchen stove, an anxious expression on his face. "We only have six more minutes."

"Are you sure you should think that long in one stretch?" Jessica asked. "You might sprain your brain or something."

Joe rolled his eyes. "Quiet, munchkins," he cried as he marked off an answer on his worksheet.

"Maybe they really are studying," Elizabeth whispered, suddenly feeling a little guilty.

"This is a whole lot more important than schoolwork," Steven said. He tossed an envelope in her direction. "Read that and then beat it. I've still got twelve questions to go."

Elizabeth pulled a letter out of the envelope and motioned for Jessica to join her. *"Dear Sir,"* she read in a low whisper while Jessica looked over her shoulder. *"Thank you for your interest in MEGA. The enclosed test will determine if you are eligible for membership in our exclusive organization."*

"What's MEGA?" Jessica asked, frowning.

"It stands for Mentally Gifted Association," Steven said with a sigh. He shoved back his chair and went over to the oven to turn off the timer. "Four and a half minutes," he told Joe. "We'll have to finish these up in my room. It's the only pest-free zone in the house."

"Steven," Elizabeth began gently, "maybe I'm wrong, but isn't MEGA only for geniuses?"

Steven nodded. "Yep. Joe and I want to join."

"Right," Jessica said sarcastically as she reached into the refrigerator for some milk. "And Elizabeth and I are going to join the Marines next week."

"You don't think I could qualify?" Steven snapped.

Elizabeth sat down at the table across from Joe. "The thing is," she said, "people with genius-level IQs are very rare."

"That's just what I told him," Joe replied.

"Joe found this ad for the MEGA test in the back of a magazine, and I bet him that I could ace it," Steven explained. "We decided we'd both take the test and see who came out on top."

"You guys are always competing over something," Jessica said. "What was it last week? Who could make the most baskets in a row without missing?"

"And yours truly won," Steven said. "Twenty-one in a row."

"And I'm never going to hear the end of it." Joe shook his head. "But I'll get even with you someday, Steven."

"I really think those IQ tests are silly," Elizabeth said thoughtfully. "There are so many different ways a person can be smart. Some people are good at taking tests, and some people are good mechanically—"

"And some people are geniuses at eating," Jessica muttered as she scanned the pantry. "Who ate all the pretzels, *Steven*?"

"We needed our strength," Steven replied. "We're using a lot of brain cells." He nodded toward the door. "Come on, Joe. Let's go up to my room and finish these. I can't wait to send them off and get the test results."

"I'll mail them on my way home," Joe volunteered.

"Does it really matter how you do?" Elizabeth asked. "I mean, do you really think some test that was advertised in the back of a magazine can tell you how smart you are?"

"Sure," Steven said. "Why not?"

"Because it's a lot more complicated than that," Elizabeth insisted.

"Besides," Jessica added, "there's no way you two are geniuses."

"Don't be too sure, Jessica," Steven warned.

"Dream on, Steven," Jessica said. "If you turn out to be a genius, I'll—" she paused, "I'll never tease you again as long as I live."

Steven grinned. "You heard her, Elizabeth!"

"I heard her, all right," Elizabeth replied, shaking her head. "But I doubt she'll have to worry about following through."

"We'll see about that," Steven crowed.

"Yeah," Joe said with a broad grin as the two boys walked away. "We'll see about that!"

On Friday afternoon, Jessica stayed after school for Boosters practice. The Boosters were the middle-school cheering squad, and most of them were also members of the Unicorn Club. The only two non-Unicorns on the squad were Amy Sutton and Winston Egbert.

Boosters practice was never very organized, but today it was going especially badly. "This new baton routine is a mess," Jessica moaned when the squad paused for a breather.

Lila nodded and wiped her forehead with the back of her arm. "So far, my baton's spent more time on the floor than in the air."

"I wish the boys' basketball team would leave," Jessica whispered to Janet. Over at the far end of the gym, several boys stood watching, bouncing their basketballs. Every time one of the Boosters made a mistake, the boys hooted and whistled.

Janet looked over at the boys. "We have the gym until four-thirty," she called. Janet was the president of the Unicorns, and also the captain of the Boosters. "Ms. Langberg said it was off-limits to you guys till then."

"Hey," Bruce Patman called back, "we're not

going to rush you. You obviously need all the practice you can get!" The other boys laughed.

"I hate it when people watch us just as we're learning a new routine," Janet muttered. "Who are all those people in the bleachers, anyway?"

Jessica followed Janet's gaze. "Those are all girlfriends of guys on the team," she said. "See? Veronica's there, and Sally Holcomb. They're not here to see us."

"Veronica follows Bruce everywhere," Lila said. "They're definitely turning into a serious couple."

"I just wish they'd go be a couple somewhere else," Janet muttered. She motioned toward the center of the gym. "Come on, everybody. Let's try this routine one more time. And Jessica, this time try not to hit my rear end with your baton."

"I didn't mean to," Jessica replied edgily. "Although it *is* an easy target to hit. Anyway, I'm used to having Ellen in between us."

"Too bad about her getting grounded," Amy said.

Lila shrugged. "At least it was only for a week."

"I still can't believe her mom's earrings didn't show up," Jessica said. "I figured the janitor would find them in the cafeteria."

"Maybe someone ate them," Lila joked.

"Hey, Boosters," Bruce yelled. "If you girls

are just going to stand around and gossip, let us have the gym!"

Janet ignored him. She clapped her hands, and the Boosters got into position for the start of their routine. "This time, let's do it right," Janet said.

But a few seconds into the routine, Jessica and Tamara Chase cartwheeled into each other and landed in a heap in the middle of the floor. Naturally, the boys burst into enthusiastic applause. "Nice work, Boosters," Charlie Cashman yelled. "Maybe you guys should change your name to the Black-and-Bluesters!"

"Hey, Jessica," Rick Hunter called. "Can we see that move again in slow motion?"

Jessica rolled her eyes. Rick, who was president of the seventh grade, was cute and popular, but he didn't seem to like Jessica much. Every time he saw her, he made it a point to tease her.

"That does it," Janet hissed. "Practice is officially over."

"It wasn't my fault," Jessica muttered as she and the other girls headed toward the bleachers to retrieve their belongings.

"Well, it sure wasn't *my* fault," Tamara shot back. "I was where I was supposed to be."

"One of those guys whistled, and it distracted me," Jessica replied. She combed her fingers through her hair. "My hair's a mess. Can I borrow your hairbrush, Janet?"

Janet reached into her purse and frowned.

"Come on, Janet," Jessica urged. "I promise my hair's clean—"

"It's gone," Janet cried. "That was my very favorite hairbrush in the world! It had natural bristles, and you know how sensitive my scalp is."

"Maybe you left it in the locker room," Amy suggested.

"No. I'm sure it was here," Janet said.

"OK," Lila cried. "Who took it?"

"My brush?" Janet asked.

"Who cares about your brush?" Lila snapped. "I want to know who took my brand-new copy of *Teenage* magazine!" She glared at the group. "It was right here under my book bag, and now it's gone."

"Wonderful," Jessica cried, dropping onto the first row of bleachers next to Amy. "I didn't even get a chance to read about Jake Sommers's engagement."

"OK, enough is enough," Lila said. "Who is the dirty rotten thief who's stealing stuff around here?"

"Maybe it's just a coincidence," Grace Oliver suggested.

"Some coincidence," Janet said. "First, Ellen's earrings disappear, now my hairbrush and Lila's magazine are missing."

"Are you sure the magazine's not here?" Jessica asked. "Maybe it fell underneath the bleachers."

"No," Lila said glumly. "I already looked."

"This *is* awfully strange," Jessica said.

"What's strange?" Veronica asked as she strolled over to join the group.

"Some of our stuff's disappeared," Lila explained. "My new *Teenage* magazine and Janet's favorite hairbrush."

Veronica's eyes widened. "Do you think someone stole them?"

"From right under our noses?" Janet asked.

"That's what happened with Ellen's earrings," Veronica pointed out.

"Maybe you guys are just losing stuff temporarily, the way I always do," Jessica suggested helpfully.

Janet scowled. "Not everyone's as irresponsible as you, Jessica. These things were definitely swiped."

Jessica shook her head. "You know, it's starting to look like Sweet Valley Middle School may actually have its very own thief!"

"Do you really think there's a Sweet Valley Swiper?" Ellen asked. It was the following Monday between second and third period, and most of the Unicorns were packed into the girls' bathroom, as usual.

"Could be," Jessica replied as she gazed at her reflection in the mirror.

"It sure would solve my problems with my mom," Ellen said. "She's making me pay for those earrings out of my allowance."

"Too bad," Jessica said sympathetically.

"Really," Veronica agreed. She was standing in front of another mirror, combing her hair. "If you ever find out who stole them, you better make their life miserable."

"That's a big if," Jessica said.

"Maybe we should try to think back over what was going on when the things were stolen," Lila suggested.

Ellen shrugged. "Why?"

"To come up with clues," Lila said. "You never know what we might figure out."

"You sound like Elizabeth after she's been reading too many of those Amanda Howard mysteries," Jessica teased. "She loves to play detective."

"This thief is probably too smart, anyway," Mandy said as she took off her wide-brimmed felt hat and began to brush her hair. "After all, he stole those things from practically right under our noses. I doubt he left any clues behind."

"Or she," Jessica said. She picked up Mandy's hat and tried it on, admiring herself in the mirror. "Great hat, Mandy," she said. "Where'd you get it?"

"Granny's Attic," Mandy replied. "It's that little antique store downtown."

"You have the greatest taste, Mandy," Veronica said, watching as Jessica set the hat down on the ledge by the mirror.

Jessica frowned. Hadn't Veronica told her almost exactly the same thing just last week? Still, she had to admit it was true. They both *did* have a way with clothes. Jessica's taste was more on the cutting edge of fashion, but Mandy had a real knack for turning thrift-store bargains into incredible outfits.

As the Unicorns headed out into the crowded hallway, Jessica paused at the bathroom door. "Coming, Veronica?" she called.

"Go ahead," Veronica said. "I'll see you in class."

"You know, Veronica's been hanging around us so much lately that I've almost started to think of her as one of the Unicorns," Jessica said as she caught up with her friends.

"Maybe she should be," Lila said. "She's perfect Unicorn material. And we all really like her."

"It doesn't hurt that she's dating Bruce Patman, either," Ellen pointed out. "That's got to be good for our image."

"Ellen," Mandy chided as the girls turned the corner. "We don't choose Unicorns on the basis of their boyfriends. I didn't have a boyfriend when I became a member."

"None of us did," Lila said. "That's what makes Veronica look especially good."

Suddenly Mandy stopped in midstride. "My hat!" she cried as her hand flew to her head. "I must have left it in the bathroom."

The girls dashed back to the bathroom. Mandy hurried over to the ledge and gasped. "Where is it? Isn't this where you left it, Jessica?"

Jessica nodded. "Right there on the ledge."

"What's wrong, Jessica?" asked Elizabeth, who was washing her hands at the far sink.

"Have you seen Mandy's hat?" Jessica asked. "You know—the dark green one with the wide brim that she had on this morning?"

Elizabeth shook her head.

"Have you seen anything at all suspicious?" Mandy asked frantically.

"Nothing," Elizabeth said. "I just got here a second ago, and the bathroom's been packed with people. It would have been easy for someone to take it."

"The Sweet Valley Swiper strikes again," Lila cried.

"Look on the bright side, Mandy," Ellen said. "At least the hat belonged to you, and not your mother."

Just then the warning bell rang. "Come on," Mandy said dejectedly. "We'd better get going or we'll be late."

"I'll keep my eyes open for any clues,

Mandy," Elizabeth said, following them to the door.

Jessica grinned at her twin. "See, Lila? What did I tell you? Elizabeth is already on the case."

The girls were halfway down the hall when Jessica spotted Veronica getting a drink at the water fountain.

"Veronica!" she called. "Did you see anyone walk off with Mandy's hat?"

"Not again! Now her hat's missing?" Veronica exclaimed. "This is really getting ridiculous! And that hat was so cute, too."

Mandy shrugged. "I know it was just a thrift-store hat, but I really liked it. Besides, my head feels naked without it. And now I've got a big ridge on my hair."

"Hey," Veronica said, reaching into her book bag. "I've got an idea. It's not nearly as cute, but—" She paused to pull out a beautiful black velvet baseball cap. "You can wear it, if you want," she said, handing it to Mandy.

"Thanks," Mandy said gratefully. "It definitely beats hat hair."

"You sure do come prepared," Elizabeth said to Veronica.

Veronica shrugged. "That hat's too big for me, anyway. You can keep it if you like it, Mandy."

"Are you sure?" Mandy asked excitedly. "This is so nice of you!"

"It's all yours," Veronica said, smiling.

Mandy put on the cap with a sigh. "This cap is great, but I'm going to find my own hat, if it's the last thing I do."

"Well, at least we know one thing," Elizabeth said. "If there had been any guys in the girls' bathroom, we definitely would have noticed. That means the thief must be a girl."

Lila nodded grimly. "Elizabeth's right. And whoever the Sweet Valley Swiper is, *she's* going to regret that she ever decided to start stealing the Unicorns' stuff!"

Three

◇

"I've been thinking about the Swiper all day," Elizabeth said as she and Jessica walked home from school that afternoon. "And I just can't figure out who she is."

"Not even Amanda Howard could solve this mystery, Elizabeth," Jessica said.

The girls turned the corner onto their tree-lined street. "Any mystery can be solved. We just have to piece together all the clues," Elizabeth said.

Jessica frowned. "The Unicorns have been trying to do that all week. Trust me. There *aren't* any clues."

"Come on," Elizabeth urged. "Don't you even want to try to figure out the mystery?"

"You're the one who loves mysteries."

"Remember back in second grade, when we had the Snoopers Club?" Elizabeth asked.

Jessica laughed. "Little kids sure can be weird. A bunch of second graders, pretending to be detectives and solve mysteries!"

"It wasn't weird," Elizabeth said defensively. The Snoopers Club was one of her favorite memories. It made her a little sad to realize that Jessica didn't feel the same way. "And we were actually pretty good detectives. I thought it was a lot of fun."

"So did I—back then. But now all that mystery stuff just seems boring."

"Not to me."

"Maybe you just have a natural aptitude for poking around into other people's business," Jessica teased, shifting her backpack from one shoulder to the other.

"Until she's caught, the Swiper's everybody's business," Elizabeth retorted. "But I guess you're right. I *do* have good instincts when it comes to solving mysteries. I solved the charm-school mystery, remember?" she said proudly. Elizabeth and her friends had managed to uncover a burglary ring involving the owners of a charm school the girls had attended.

Jessica grinned. "Well, it took you a while, but I have to admit you did figure it out eventually. Who knows? Maybe eventually you'll solve the mystery of the Sweet Valley Swiper, too. Personally, I think all the missing stuff will turn up sooner or later. That's what always happens when my stuff disappears."

"Mine, too, I hope," Elizabeth said, giving Jessica a sidelong glance. "I don't suppose you've found my missing sweater yet?"

Suddenly, they heard the noise of two bicycles whizzing down the street at high speed. "Make way, midgets," Steven called.

"I wonder what he and Joe are in such a hurry for?" Jessica said as the two boys rode by in a blur. "Let's go see."

"Jessica," Elizabeth said sternly. "Before you change the subject, about my sweater—"

"You're the super snooper," Jessica said nonchalantly. "I'm sure you'll find it . . . eventually."

When Jessica and Elizabeth arrived home, they found Joe and Steven in the family room. Steven was holding a long white envelope.

"So go ahead, open it," Joe urged. "It can't be any worse than mine."

"What is it, Steven?" Elizabeth asked.

"It's his score from the MEGA test," Joe explained. "Mine was waiting in the mailbox when I got home."

"That was why they were speeding over

here," Jessica said. "Steven couldn't wait to find out how stupid he is."

"It sure didn't take long to get your test results," Elizabeth said. "You just mailed them off a week ago."

"They're computerized tests," Joe reminded Elizabeth. "They don't take long to score."

Steven held the envelope up to the light.

"Do it already, Wakefield," Joe said impatiently. "I've been humiliated. Now it's your turn."

"Humiliated?" Elizabeth asked as she set down her backpack and sat on the couch. "What do you mean, Joe?"

Joe reached into his jeans pocket and pulled out a folded letter. "My score was just average," he said with a sigh. "Can you believe it?"

"No," Jessica replied, giggling. "You must have cheated."

Joe crumpled up his letter and tossed it at Jessica. "If I wanted this kind of abuse, I'd go home and talk to Janet."

Elizabeth noticed that Steven was looking rather apprehensive. "You know, you could just throw the envelope away, Steven," she suggested. She hated to see him embarrassed over something as silly and pointless as an IQ test. "After all, this is a ridiculous way to judge people."

"No way," Joe protested. "Steven *has* to open his. I opened mine."

Steven shrugged. "Elizabeth's right, Joe. This is a stupid way to judge a person's intelligence." He slit open the envelope and pulled out the letter. "So no matter what it says—" He stopped in mid-sentence, and suddenly his expression changed. "I *knew* it," he cried happily, tossing the letter into the air. "Read it and weep!"

"What does it say?" Joe demanded.

Elizabeth picked up the letter off the floor. *"Dear Sir,"* she read out loud. *"We are very pleased to inform you of your acceptance into the exclusive MEGA organization. You scored in the 99.99th percentile, which places you in the category of a genius Intelligence Quoshent."* Elizabeth looked up. "This is so strange—" she began.

"I'll say," Jessica muttered. "I thought computers weren't supposed to make mistakes, but this one obviously made a whopper!"

"No," Elizabeth said, shaking her head. "That's not what I meant. What's strange is that they misspelled *quotient.*"

"So?" Jessica said. "Lots of very smart people are lousy spellers."

"It was probably just a clerical error," Joe said, grabbing the letter from Elizabeth.

Steven crossed his arms over his chest and gave Joe a superior smile. "What exactly are you referring to? The misspelling, or my score?"

"They could both be mistakes," Joe said. His eyes lit up. "For all we know, they mixed up our scores! Maybe *I'm* the genius, and you're just Mr. Average."

Steven shook his head. "Face it, Joe. Your best friend just happens to be a genius."

"This isn't possible," Jessica argued. "If you're a genius, how come you don't bring home straight A-pluses from school?"

"Maybe I'm just not applying myself," Steven said smugly. "Besides, I do get good grades."

"But not *great* grades," Jessica pointed out.

Joe sighed. "Believe me, Jessica, I'd like to agree with you," he said. "But these tests are very accurate. And computers don't make mistakes."

"That's a good point, Joe," Steven said gleefully. "Not bad for a non-genius."

"A minute ago, you agreed that a test like this was a stupid way to judge intelligence," Jessica reminded her brother.

"A minute ago, I had no idea how intelligent I was," Steven replied.

"I don't know," Elizabeth said thoughtfully. "I mean, the fact that you scored well on one test doesn't really change anything."

Steven's eyes widened. "It changes everything, Elizabeth! I'm a genius. This means I have all kinds of untapped mental power I never even dreamed of." He glanced over at Jessica, who was making a face. "And even more important, it means that Jessica will have to keep her vow never to tease me again as long as she lives."

"I was afraid you'd remember that," Jessica muttered.

"I'm a genius, Jessica," Steven replied smugly. "I remember everything."

"Where's Steven?" Mrs. Wakefield asked that evening as the family sat down to dinner.

"The last time I saw him, he was upstairs gloating," Jessica replied, reaching for the salad bowl.

"Gloating over what?" Mr. Wakefield asked.

"Haven't you heard?" Jessica asked. "Steven took an IQ test. Turns out he's a genius."

Mrs. Wakefield grinned. "Just what kind of test was this?"

"It's from some organization called MEGA," Elizabeth answered. "He and Joe sent for tests. They just got their scores back this afternoon."

"I'm not sure that a mail-in test is the most reliable way to gauge intelligence," Mr. Wakefield said doubtfully.

"The MEGA test is extremely reliable, Dad," Steven said as he entered the dining room. He was wearing a pair of glasses and carrying a large red book.

Jessica stared at him in disbelief. "Since when do you wear glasses, Steven?" She peered across the table as he sat down. "Wait a minute. Those are *my* old glasses!"

"Precisely, dear sibling," Steven said in a very

sophisticated-sounding voice. He removed the glasses and set them on the table next to his milk. "I was just striving to attain a countenance that reflects my newfound intellectual capacity."

Jessica cast a confused look at Elizabeth. "What's he talking about?"

"I think he's trying to look smarter."

"Steven," Mr. Wakefield said, leaning forward, "just where do you think this newfound intellectual capacity comes from?"

"He went to Brains-R-Us," Jessica answered with a smirk.

"No editorial comment is necessary, Jessica," Mr. Wakefield warned. "My point is, a test doesn't make you smart, Steven. It merely confirms what was already there."

"A point well taken," Steven said smoothly. "But discovering I'm a genius has made me realize that I need to tap into my real potential, Dad."

"Is that why you're carrying around one of my law books?"

"I thought perhaps we could have a discussion of torts after dinner," Steven said.

"Tortes?" Jessica repeated. "Isn't that a kind of cake?"

"Silly Jessica," Steven said, clucking his tongue. "A tort is a legal term."

"Well, ex*cuse* me," Jessica exclaimed. "When exactly did you get your law degree, Steven?"

"When you have an IQ like mine, you just absorb information like a sponge."

Mrs. Wakefield passed a bowl of mashed potatoes to Steven. "Even if this test is accurate, honey, does it really matter? I mean, you've always been an excellent student—"

"Of *course* it matters," Steven exclaimed. "It's opened up whole new worlds for me. Think of what I've been missing. Physics! Astronomy! Chemistry! Classical music! Great literature!"

Jessica pointed at Steven. "Look. I want to know where my brother is, and what you've done with him."

"I know what you're thinking, Jessica," Steven said. "You're wondering if I'll still talk to you little people now that I'm a genius."

"Actually, I'm wondering if you'll do my homework for me, now that you're a genius," Jessica shot back.

"Well," Mrs. Wakefield said, glancing at her husband. "If this test gets Steven more interested in some of the subjects he mentioned, what harm could there be?"

"None, I suppose," Mr. Wakefield said. He grinned at Steven. "Just don't let it go to your head."

"I think it may be too late for that, Dad," Elizabeth said with a smile.

* * *

"I hate playing volleyball against you, Lila," Jessica muttered on Tuesday after gym class, stomping up to her locker.

"Why? Because my team won?" Lila asked with a grin.

"Because you cheat," Jessica complained.

"How can you cheat at volleyball?" Elizabeth asked.

"Lila spikes the ball over the net too hard." Jessica held out her hands. "My palms are bright red from hitting it back. I'm getting a huge blister."

"Is that where you've been since the end of class?" Lila asked as she ran a comb through her hair. "Getting a Band-Aid from Ms. Langberg for your blister?"

"Don't laugh, Lila. It's a huge blister," Jessica exclaimed. "Want to see?"

"Gee, Jessica, it's a tempting offer," Lila said sarcastically, "but I think I'll pass—" Suddenly she stopped when someone nearby let out a scream.

"That sounded like Mandy," Jessica said.

The girls hurried over to the next row of lockers. They found Mandy sitting on a bench in front of her open locker. "Not again," she moaned.

"Mandy, what's wrong?" Jessica asked.

"It's gone," Mandy said. "My jean jacket! It was right here a minute ago."

"It was stolen?" Elizabeth asked.

"First my hat, and now my jacket," Mandy said grimly. "This is really getting out of control."

"The Swiper strikes again," Jessica said. "Too bad, too. I really loved that jacket, Mandy. Just this morning I was telling you how much I liked that great embroidery on it, remember?"

"That's one good thing," Elizabeth pointed out. "If the thief tries to wear the jacket anywhere, we'll recognize it."

"Did you leave your locker unlocked during class?" Lila asked Mandy.

"I just unlocked it a minute ago when we came in, and then I went to the bathroom. When I got back . . ." Her voice trailed off.

"This is terrible," Veronica said as she joined the group. "It's getting so you can't trust people anymore."

"Tell me about it," Ellen cried, storming over. "Whoever swiped my deodorant is going to be awfully sorry!"

"Not as sorry as the rest of us," Jessica said.

"Joke all you want, Jessica. It was that baby-powder-scent spray you're always borrowing," Ellen said.

"Now the thief's really gone too far," Lila commented, pinching her nose. "Maybe you two should sit somewhere else for lunch."

"Let's see," Elizabeth said thoughtfully. "So far, the victims have been Ellen, Lila, Janet, and Mandy. Has anybody else had anything stolen?"

"Just you," Jessica joked. "If you count that sweater you're missing."

Elizabeth smiled. "As far as we know, that wasn't the Swiper," she said. "This means that so far, only Unicorns have been affected."

"That's a good point, Elizabeth," Veronica said as she sat down on the bench in front of her locker and pulled off her sneakers.

"So what does that tell us?" Jessica asked.

"I don't know . . . yet," Elizabeth said, tapping a finger on her chin. "Give me a while to think about it."

"I'm not sure we should wait a while," Mandy said. "I've been thinking that maybe we should report all these thefts to Mr. Clark."

"What can Mr. Clark do?" Veronica asked. "He can't exactly guard everyone's lockers all day —especially not in here."

Mandy smiled wryly. "Maybe not, but I still think it would be a good idea to tell him what's going on."

"Mandy's right," Elizabeth agreed. "If he tells all the teachers, maybe there's a chance the thief will get caught red-handed."

Veronica shook her head. "I just don't see what good it'll do."

"Probably none," Mandy said. "But what else can we do?"

"I know what *I'm* going to do," Lila proclaimed. "I'm going to watch my stuff like a hawk, every second of the day. I may even stop wearing expensive jewelry to school."

"I didn't know you owned any cheap jewelry," Jessica teased. She pointed to Lila's Watchman, which was lying beside her purse. "If you need any help keeping an eye on your Watchman, just let me know. I'm available for baby-sitting duty."

"Especially this afternoon, during *Days of Turmoil*, right?" Lila said sarcastically. "Forget it, Jessica. No one's getting their hands on this Watchman. Not even you. And certainly not the Sweet Valley Swiper—whoever she is!"

Whoever she is, Elizabeth repeated to herself. The more she watched this mystery unfold, the more she felt certain she could get to the bottom of it.

Four

◇

That afternoon, right after the final bell had rung, Elizabeth and Jessica were walking down the hall when they noticed Veronica slumped against her locker.

"That does it," she moaned. "Now *I've* been swiped!"

"What did she take?" Elizabeth asked, rushing over.

"Only my very favorite notebook in the entire world," Veronica said bitterly. "The one with the picture of Jake Sommers on the cover."

"When did you first notice it was missing?" Elizabeth asked.

"Just now, when I went to put it away in my locker," Veronica replied. "I know I had it in Mr.

Seigel's class. Jessica was admiring it, remember, Jess?"

Jessica nodded. "I told her it was bound to become a collector's item now that Jake's engaged."

Lila and Ellen walked up to them. "What's wrong, Veronica?" Lila asked.

"Another one bites the dust," Jessica said. "Veronica just got robbed."

"So it's not just Unicorns anymore," Lila said to Elizabeth.

"Well, Veronica's an *almost* Unicorn," Jessica said.

Veronica blushed. "Thanks, Jessica. I can't tell you how special that makes me feel," she said in a sugary-sweet voice that sounded so insincere Elizabeth rolled her eyes. *Cut it out, Elizabeth,* she chided herself instantly. *You promised Jessica that you'd give Veronica the benefit of the doubt.*

Just then Bruce strolled up. "Anything wrong, Veronica?" he asked, slipping his arm around her waist.

"Somebody stole my notebook," Veronica said with a pout.

"So the Sweet Valley Swiper's still at it, huh?" Bruce said with a laugh.

"It's not funny, Bruce," Elizabeth said. "All kinds of things have been stolen."

"Just girl stuff, from what I hear," Bruce said

with a shrug. "A brush, a hat . . . I mean, big deal."

"It is a big deal. Today the Swiper even took my deodorant," Ellen cried.

"Well, then," Bruce said, nodding solemnly. "That *is* serious. Especially since I have to sit next to you in social studies." He squeezed Veronica's hand. "Want me to walk you home?"

"Well . . ." Veronica hesitated. "I do, but first I think maybe we should go to Mr. Clark's office and tell him about the Swiper."

Elizabeth frowned. "You told Mandy you thought going to Mr. Clark was a dumb idea."

"That was before I lost my Jake Sommers notebook," Veronica said sharply.

"Why do you need Jake Sommers, when you already have me?" Bruce said with a broad grin.

"There's Mr. Clark now," Jessica said. "Over there, in the lobby."

The group dashed down the emptying hallway and caught up with Mr. Clark. "Please, people," he exclaimed, holding up a warning hand. "No running."

"But this is important," Jessica cried.

"The Unicorns keep getting robbed," Lila explained. "So far, we've lost earrings, a hat, a jean jacket—"

"Deodorant," Ellen added.

"You've *lost* them, you say?" Mr. Clark said.

"Maybe you should check the lost and found. They might just have been misplaced."

"That's what I think happened," Jessica said. "I lose stuff all the time."

"No," Veronica said firmly. "Somebody stole my notebook. I didn't lose it."

"I already checked the lost and found, Mr. Clark," Ellen said. "Nothing's there but a few pens and one scuzzy sneaker."

Mr. Clark thought for a moment. "Tell you what. Why don't you girls go into the office and give Mrs. Knight a complete list of all the missing items? In the meantime, I'll pass along this information to the faculty, so they can be on the lookout for—what did you call him?"

"The Swiper," Jessica answered.

"We think it's a girl, because some of the missing items were stolen from the girls' bathroom and the girls' locker room," Elizabeth added.

"I may also mention this tomorrow morning during announcements, so the other students can be aware of what's been happening," Mr. Clark said.

"Couldn't you call the police?" Ellen suggested, "or the FBI?"

Jessica rolled her eyes. "Yeah, right. I'm sure the FBI is going to drop everything to search for your missing deodorant."

"*You* weren't the one who got grounded for a

week, Jessica," Ellen said defensively. "My mom was really mad about her earrings."

Mr. Clark cleared his throat. "All I can tell you is to keep a close eye on your belongings until we catch the Swiper. And when we catch her . . . well, I'll deal with that when the time comes."

When the twins reached home, they found Joe ringing the front doorbell. "Hey, midgets," he said. "Is Steven home yet? He rushed out of class so fast, I didn't even see him leave."

"How would we know?" Jessica said. "We just got here." She grinned at Elizabeth. "No wonder Joe flunked his IQ test."

Elizabeth started to open the door, but Joe held up a hand. "Listen," he whispered. "Have you noticed anything, uh . . . strange about Steven lately?"

"Steven's always been strange," Jessica replied.

Suddenly, a long, plaintive shriek filled the air.

"What's that noise?" Joe demanded.

"Search me," Jessica said. "But it's coming from Steven's room."

"It sounds like a wolf howling at the top of its lungs," Joe said, covering his ears.

Elizabeth grinned as she opened the door. "I have a feeling that wolf is actually an opera singer, Joe."

"Hi, girls," Mrs. Wakefield called from the kitchen. "Do me a favor, will you? Run upstairs and tell your brother to turn down the music. I'm pleased to see him taking an interest in opera, but my ears would appreciate it if he took a little *less* interest!"

When Joe and the twins reached Steven's room, they stopped dead in their tracks, staring through the doorway in disbelief. While the music blared from his CD player, Steven sat mesmerized in front of a chess board that was set up on his desk. He moved a piece one space, then jumped up from his chair and ran to the other side of the desk, where he'd placed another chair. He sat down, examined the board for a moment, and then moved another piece. Then he jumped up again and ran back to the first chair. He was so absorbed in the game that he didn't even notice he had company.

Joe cleared his throat and Steven looked up in surprise. "Hello, *mes amis*," Steven said loudly, his voice barely audible over the noise of the CD player. "Enter, please."

"What did you call us?" Jessica yelled.

Steven reached for the volume control and quieted the screaming soprano. "*Mes amis*," he said. "French for friends, dear sibling."

"See what I mean?" Joe asked under his breath. He sat down on the edge of Steven's bed. "What's that you're listening to, old buddy?"

"An opera by Richard Wagner I just bought," Steven replied. "If you want, I could start it over from the beginning, so you could hear it all the way through—"

"No way," Joe said with a groan. "I'd rather listen to fingernails on a blackboard."

"Joe," Steven said with a condescending smile, "you've got to learn to expand your musical horizons. There's more to life than MTV."

"Since when do you know anything about opera?" Jessica asked skeptically.

"I just never realized what a refined ear I have for music," Steven explained. He gave Joe a grateful smile. "I can't thank you enough for suggesting we take that IQ test, Joe. I've said it before and I'll say it again—it's opened up whole new worlds for me."

"Yeah, well, I was hoping you might want to spend a little time with me in *this* world this afternoon. You know—playing a little basketball?"

Steven threw back his head and laughed. "Don't be silly, Joe. Competitive sports are just a mindless display of the baser animal instincts."

Joe cast the twins a plaintive look.

"Don't ask me," Jessica said with a shrug. "Elizabeth is the only one around here who can translate."

"Steven, just because you've found new interests doesn't mean that you have to give up things you enjoy, like basketball," Elizabeth argued.

"Calculating the trajectory of a spheroid object through space no longer interests me," Steven replied airily.

"He says he doesn't want to shoot hoops anymore," Elizabeth translated.

"It's hardly what I'd call intellectually stimulating," Steven added with a dismissive wave of his hand.

"No," Joe agreed. "It's what you used to call *fun.*"

"Perhaps you'll allow me to introduce you to the fascinating world of chess," Steven said.

"That's Dad's chess set. You don't play chess," Jessica reminded Steven.

"Correction, dear sibling—"

"Would you *please* stop calling me that?" Jessica yelled.

"When did you learn to play chess, Steven?" Elizabeth asked.

"Last night," Steven replied. "I glanced over the rules for five minutes, and lo and behold, a chess master was born."

"But real chess masters take years to perfect their game," Elizabeth said.

"It's all a matter of the wattage upstairs," Steven replied, pointing to his head.

"Well, if you ask me, there's a real dim bulb burning in your attic," Jessica shot back.

"Steven," Elizabeth said gently, "don't you

think maybe you're taking this whole genius thing a little too far?''

Steven just shrugged and turned his attention back to his chess set.

"Is he like this at school, too?" Jessica whispered.

"Not as bad," Joe replied.

"At school I am striving, as best I can, not to alienate my peers, with their inferior brains," Steven said, sounding hurt. "Here, at home, and with my best friend, I had hoped I could relax and be my true self." He sighed heavily.

"Of course I want you to be your true self, Steven," Joe said. "But doesn't that true self include the old Steven? You know—the guy who never passed up a chance to shoot some hoops?"

Steven sighed again. "Here," he said, holding up one of the chess pieces. "This is called a knight, Joe."

Joe crossed his arms over his chest. "Forget it. I'll play basketball solo."

"Perhaps it's for the best," Steven admitted reluctantly. "What challenge would there be in my playing chess with someone who's merely of average intellect? Besides, I really prefer my own company." He set the knight down and moved a pawn forward a space.

"I'm just a mere mortal," Jessica said, heading for the door, "but I believe that may have been a hint for us to beat it."

"You're welcome to stay," Steven murmured as he moved from one chair to the other, his eyes glued to the chess board. "There's a wonderful aria coming up."

"Aria?" Jessica repeated.

"A song in the opera."

"Thanks," Joe said, rising. "I'll take a rain check."

"I wish you'd never given Steven that stupid test, Joe," Jessica complained when they were safely in the hallway.

Joe smiled. "I've definitely created a monster, haven't I?"

"Frankenbrain," Jessica said. "If he keeps this up, somebody's going to have to teach him a lesson."

"Maybe somebody will, Jessica," Joe said. "You never know."

"Hi, Elizabeth. What are you doing?" Jessica asked that evening as she walked into Elizabeth's bedroom.

Elizabeth looked up from her desk. "The same thing you're supposed to be doing—our history homework." She held up a worksheet. "Do you remember when Abraham Lincoln was shot?"

"Lizzie, I've got more important things on my mind," Jessica said, tapping her foot. "We're going to have to do something about Steven."

"Like what?" Elizabeth asked, setting aside her book.

"I don't know." Jessica sat down on the edge of Elizabeth's bed. "Isn't there some kind of operation you can have to make you less intelligent? If so, Steven needs it. He just walked past my room, talking to himself."

"So?"

"So, he was talking in *German*, Elizabeth! He told me he's learning a bunch of different languages at once, just for the fun of it."

"I know he's getting a little carried away," Elizabeth said. "But there's nothing wrong with Steven being interested in new things."

"But it's like he's had a personality transplant," Jessica complained. "He was obnoxious before, but this is an even more annoying kind of obnoxious!" She stood up and reached for a notepad that was sitting on the corner of Elizabeth's desk. "What's this?"

"Notes for our history test next week."

"No. Here, in the margins."

Elizabeth smiled. "I was just doodling. Trying to put together clues about the Swiper."

Jessica raised her eyebrows. "And?"

"And there aren't any, as far as I can see. I'm stumped."

"Stumped by what, dear sibling?" Steven asked, suddenly appearing in the doorway.

"I warned you, Steven," Jessica growled. "Can the *dear sibling* stuff."

"Somebody's been stealing things at school," Elizabeth explained to Steven. "We call her the Sweet Valley Swiper. But so far, no one has a clue who it is."

Steven leaned against the wall, pursing his lips. "It's elementary, my dear—"

"Steven!" Jessica shouted.

"I think he was going to say *Watson* this time, Jessica," Elizabeth said with a grin.

"What you need to do is establish motive," Steven said. "And the rest will follow, as night follows day."

Jessica let out a groan. "Geez, Steven. I know you're a genius, but do you have to go around *sounding* like one every second of the day?"

Steven's face fell. "I'm sorry, dear—um, Jessica. Really. But it's hard finding out you're—you know, *different* from everyone else. It's really very lonely. I couldn't stand it if I gained a bigger brain but lost you munchkins."

Jessica sighed. Steven looked so sad and hurt, she felt lousy. It hadn't occurred to her he might be having a hard time adjusting to his new, brainier self.

"That's OK, Steven," she said gently. "You know we'll stick by you, no matter how obnoxious you get."

"Thanks, Jessica," Steven said gratefully.

"You know, having a genius brother isn't all bad."
He reached for Elizabeth's history worksheet. "I'll
show you what I mean. Question number seven,
on Lincoln's assassination. The answer's 1865.
April fourteenth, if I recall correctly." He closed
his eyes. "No, wait," he said, opening them. "Lincoln was shot on April fourteenth, but he died on
April fifteenth."

"How do you know that?" Jessica exclaimed.

"It's all tucked away up here," Steven said,
tapping his forehead. "I've just started realizing
how much data I've got stored away. It's a little
like being a computer."

"A computer with a very large appetite,"
Elizabeth joked.

"Touché, dear sibling." Steven glanced over at
Jessica with a nervous smile. "Oops. Sorry."

"That's OK," Jessica said. "I guess I'm just
going to have to get used to the new, improved
Steven." She grabbed Elizabeth's worksheet. "And
since you're in the mood to be helpful, maybe you
could answer number eight, while you're at it."

Steven held up a warning finger. "That
wouldn't be fair, Jessica," he said. "You've got to
learn to work up to your own potential." He
grinned. "Even if it *is* limited."

Jessica reached for Elizabeth's pillow and
threw it at Steven, but he was already out the
door.

* * *

"What are you writing, Elizabeth?" Amy asked at lunch the following day.

Elizabeth looked up from her notebook. "I was making a list of everything that's been stolen so far by the Swiper. You know—to see if I could find any clues."

"I hope they find her soon," Amy said as she unwrapped her sandwich. "Ever since Mr. Clark made that announcement about the Swiper over the intercom this morning, people have been acting *very* strangely."

Elizabeth nodded. "They're all afraid they might be the next victim. Look at the people over there in the lunch line. Ellen must be carrying everything she owns with her. She's got all her books, and she's wearing her coat. And this morning, in homeroom, a couple of girls told me they were going to stop wearing jewelry to school."

"You can't be too careful," said Leslie Forsythe, who was sitting a few seats down from Elizabeth and Amy. "I'm standing guard over Winston's sandwich while he gets some milk."

"That *is* getting awfully paranoid," Amy exclaimed.

"Not really," Leslie replied. "Have you ever had one of Winston's tuna guacamoles on rye? They're incredible."

Elizabeth laughed. "Everyone's acting weird, but no one's doing anything to find the Swiper."

Amy shrugged. "We may just have to wait until the Swiper makes a mistake."

"That's not what the Snoopers would have done," Elizabeth said with a sly grin.

Amy laughed. "Remember all the cases we solved?" she asked. "I really miss those days."

"Amy," Elizabeth said, leaning across the table. "What would you think about reviving the Snoopers, just long enough to solve this case?"

Amy grinned. "I'm game. But this isn't going to be an easy case to crack. We don't have any real clues."

Elizabeth nodded. "I know. But that's my favorite kind of case. For the time being, let's just keep our eyes open. For all we know, the Swiper could be right here, under our very noses."

She glanced over just as Leslie sneaked a bite of Winston's sandwich. "Hey, don't look at me," Leslie said with a guilty smile. "Just because I have a big appetite doesn't mean I'm a thief!"

Five

◇

"Jessica," Lila whispered loudly during roll call in homeroom Thursday morning. "Take a look at this."

Jessica twisted around in her seat, and Lila held up her Watchman. "It's Jake Sommers on the *Good Morning, Sweet Valley* show," Lila exclaimed. "His fiancée is with him!"

Jessica grabbed the television and tried to yank it out of Lila's hands. "Let me see," she said. "I've got to see what she looks like!"

"Hey, give it back, Jessica!" Lila cried, leaning back in her chair and pulling.

"Ladies?" Mr. Davis said irritably. "Is there some reason you feel compelled to wrestle first thing in the morning?"

"My money's on Jessica to win," Winston joked.

Mr. Davis marched over to the girls. Jessica let go of the Watchman and sank down into her seat.

"Would this brawl have anything to do with that miniature TV on your desk?" Mr. Davis asked Lila.

"Jessica was trying to steal it from me," Lila said, clutching the Watchman to her chest protectively.

"Hand it over, Lila," Mr. Davis commanded.

"But I can't!" Lila exclaimed.

Mr. Davis cleared his throat. "Excuse me?" he said sternly.

"The Swiper's on the loose, Mr. Davis," Lila argued. "It's too dangerous."

"Trust me, Lila. I'll put it in my desk drawer for safekeeping until the end of class."

"But—"

"It'll be OK, Lila," Veronica whispered from her seat across the aisle.

"You can keep it, if you insist," Mr. Davis said. "And watch it all the way to Mr. Clark's office. I'm sure he'd be interested in seeing the latest TV technology."

"Oh, all right," Lila growled. She made a face at Jessica. "This is all your fault, Jessica."

"I just wanted to see Jake," Jessica muttered. *And I would have, too, if Lila weren't so selfish*, she added to herself resentfully.

"Interesting gadget," Mr. Davis murmured as he placed the Watchman in his desk drawer. He gave Lila a warning look. "But very disruptive. And speaking of disruptive, Jessica, do something with that gum you keep snapping. It's giving me a headache."

Jessica swallowed her gum and sighed. While Mr. Clark droned on over the intercom, reading the morning announcements, she fell into a pleasant daydream about Jake and his upcoming marriage. He and his fiancée were going to honeymoon on a private island in the Caribbean, then settle into a huge house in Hollywood. It was so romantic!

When the bell rang, she looked up in surprise. Mr. Davis was busy erasing the blackboard, and most of the class was already streaming down the aisles and out the door. Jessica grabbed her books and ran to join the others. She'd just passed Mr. Davis's desk when she heard Lila cry out.

"It's gone?" Lila shrieked. "What do you mean, it's gone?"

Jessica turned around to see Mr. Davis staring into his desk drawer, a mystified expression on his face. "I can't imagine what happened, Lila. I put it right here. Someone must have reached in and grabbed it while my back was turned. Did you see anything?"

"No!" Lila cried. "This is horrible!"

"I absolutely agree," Mr. Davis said. "But

don't worry, Lila. I'm sure we'll get to the bottom of this. Someone must have seen something."

"Too bad, Lila," Jessica said sympathetically.

"This never would have happened if you could have kept your grubby paws off it!" Lila cried.

"Now, Lila," Mr. Davis said in a reasonable voice. "It's not Jessica's fault—"

"I don't care whose fault it is! All I care about is getting my Watchman back!"

"Lila, what happened?" Veronica asked, sticking her head in the doorway.

"Her Watchman was stolen," Jessica said.

"You're kidding!" Veronica cried. "Right here, in the middle of class?"

"I'm going to go file a report with Mr. Clark immediately," Mr. Davis said.

"He won't find it," Lila snapped. "He can't even find Ellen's deodorant. I'm going to call my dad and have him get in touch with the police." She snapped her fingers. "No! I'm going to have him hire my very own private investigator!"

"Lila, you don't need to do that," Veronica said, rushing over to her side. "We're bound to find out who the Swiper is soon."

"How?" Lila wailed.

Veronica hesitated. "I don't know," she replied. "But something will come up. You know— some kind of clue." She paused. "Who knows? Maybe someone will come forward and admit they saw the thief." She patted Lila's arm. "Really. I'm sure your Watchman will turn up."

Lila took a deep breath. "Thanks. You're a good friend, Veronica," she said. She scowled at Jessica. "Unlike *some* people I know."

"I'm sure this will blow over, Jessica," Mr. Davis said in a comforting voice as Lila and Veronica marched away. "Lila will calm down soon."

"You don't know Lila," Jessica said, shaking her head.

"Any new Swiper clues?" Amy asked Elizabeth that afternoon as they walked down the hall. The final bell had just rung, and the hall was packed with students shouting and rushing for the doors.

Elizabeth shook her head. "After I heard about Lila's Watchman, I asked around, but no one in Mr. Davis's homeroom noticed anything unusual this morning."

"Everybody always rushes straight for the door at the end of homeroom. I'm not really surprised that no one saw anything."

At the far end of the hall, Elizabeth saw Jessica putting some books into her locker. "Poor Jessica," she said. "She told me Lila's been giving her a hard time all day about trying to borrow the Watchman during homeroom—"

Suddenly someone came barreling down the

hallway at high speed, nearly knocking Amy and Elizabeth over.

"What was that?" Elizabeth demanded.

"You mean *who*," Amy said looking over her shoulder. "It was Lila, and she's heading straight for Jessica."

Elizabeth turned and watched Lila storm over to Jessica's locker. Lila's face was beet red with fury, and Elizabeth noticed that she was clutching a small piece of paper.

"Come on, Amy," Elizabeth urged. "I have the feeling Jessica may need some moral support. Not to mention a couple of bodyguards."

"Jessica Wakefield," Lila screamed. "I can't believe you would do something like this! And you're supposed to be my friend!"

Jessica shook her head, looking confused. "Lila, I told you I was sorry about what happened in homeroom, but I don't see why you have to have a conniption fit over it—"

"I'll show you what happened in homeroom," Lila cried, so loudly that students in the hallway stopped and turned to see what was happening.

Lila lunged toward Jessica's locker, pushing Jessica out of the way. "What happened in homeroom is that you stole my Watchman!"

"Lila, you must be kidding!" Jessica protested. "Have you lost your mind?"

"No," Lila yelled, "but you've definitely lost

a friend!" She reached into the messy top shelf of Jessica's locker and fished around. Suddenly she withdrew her hand and held something up for everyone to see. "My Watchman!" she cried triumphantly.

"But . . ." Jessica's voice trailed off. "But . . . Lila, I—I didn't take it! I have no idea how it got there!"

Lila spun on her heel without a word. She paused in front of Elizabeth. "Please inform your twin that I am never speaking to her again."

"Lila, I'm sure there's a logical explanation," Elizabeth said, glancing over at her sister, who stood in front of her locker with a bewildered expression on her face. "You know Jessica better than this."

"I *thought* I did," Lila said, shooting Jessica an angry look.

"What's all the shouting out here?"

They all turned to see Mrs. Arnette, their social-studies teacher, walking toward them.

Lila thrust the Watchman in Mrs. Arnette's face. "Look what I found in Jessica's locker!"

Mrs. Arnette looked from Lila to Jessica and back again. "Is that the little TV that Mr. Davis said was stolen from you today?"

"It *was* stolen," Lila muttered. "By my best friend. I mean, my *ex*-best friend."

"I didn't steal it, Mrs. Arnette," Jessica cried. "I swear. I know this looks bad—"

Mrs. Arnette nodded gravely and reached for Jessica's arm. "You're right about that, young lady," she said grimly. "It looks very bad."

Elizabeth and Amy waited outside Mr. Clark's office for Jessica. "She's been in there a long time," Amy whispered nervously after a half hour had passed.

"Poor Jessica," Elizabeth said. Jessica had gotten into plenty of scrapes before, but Elizabeth couldn't ever remember seeing her twin look so scared. "I wish I could be in there with her, to help defend her."

"What could you say to defend her?" Amy asked gently. "I mean, the TV was right there in her locker."

Elizabeth sighed. "I realize it looks bad. But you know Jessica. Sure, she gets into trouble sometimes, but she's not a thief."

"Still," Amy argued, "how do you explain it?"

"I can't," Elizabeth admitted. She'd been asking herself the same question. The evidence was awfully convincing. It was possible someone had planted the Watchman in Jessica's locker, but Jessica always kept it locked. No one knew the combination—not even Elizabeth.

Amy shook her head. "You have to admit, this doesn't look good for Jessica at all."

"She's my sister, Amy," Elizabeth said firmly.

"And as far as I'm concerned, Jessica is innocent until proven guilty."

Just then Mr. Clark's office door opened, and Jessica stepped out, followed by Mrs. Arnette and Mr. Clark.

"Jessica!" Elizabeth exclaimed, rising out of her chair. She looked up at Mr. Clark and then back to Jessica. "Can, uh, you go now?"

"Not quite yet, Elizabeth," Mr. Clark said seriously. "Jessica's agreed to show us the contents of her locker."

"But why?" Elizabeth asked.

"To look for all the other stuff that's missing," Jessica said sullenly. "They think I'm the Swiper."

"Mr. Clark, I know there's an explanation for this," Elizabeth cried.

"I wish there were," Mr. Clark replied. "Stealing is a very serious offense. It could even result in suspension."

"But I'm sure Jessica's innocent," Elizabeth argued, even though, in her heart, she had to admit she wasn't completely convinced herself.

"Thanks, Elizabeth, but don't bother. I already tried," Jessica said in a resigned voice.

Jessica led the way down the empty hallway, followed by Mr. Clark, Mrs. Arnette, Elizabeth, and Amy. When she reached her locker, her hands were trembling so badly that it took her three tries before she could open it.

Elizabeth held her breath while Mr. Clark

rummaged through Jessica's locker, searching for the other missing items. *If the Watchman was there, there's no telling what else he'll find,* she thought to herself. *Either because someone planted them there, or* . . . Instantly she felt a wave of shame wash over her. How could she doubt her own twin sister this way?

After several minutes, Mr. Clark stepped back. "No sign of the other missing items," he reported.

"Now what?" Jessica asked.

Mr. Clark exchanged a look with Mrs. Arnette. "Well, the fact that the other missing items aren't here doesn't prove your innocence, Jessica. The most expensive stolen item *was* here, after all. I'm going to have to think about this for a while." Mr. Clark rubbed his forehead. "In the meantime, if you do come up with an explanation, I'd love to hear it."

Jessica sighed. "So would I," she said under her breath.

Elizabeth looked at Amy. "So would we," she whispered.

"Time to face my doom," Jessica muttered as the twins arrived home that afternoon.

"What do you mean?" Elizabeth asked.

"I'm going to call all the Unicorns and see how much damage has been done to my reputation," Jessica replied.

"Jess," Elizabeth said, "you know how rumors are. Some people are bound to jump to the wrong conclusion, but your true friends will always stick by you."

"We'll see," Jessica said grimly.

They headed for the family room, where Steven was watching TV. "Can you turn it down a little?" Jessica asked irritably. "I have to make some important phone calls. Besides, I thought TV was beneath someone with your intelligence."

"But this is public television, dear sibling," Steven protested. "They're doing a riveting special on the mating habits of the porcupine."

Jessica scowled. "*Steven.*"

"I can tape it, I suppose," Steven said, getting up. He clicked on the VCR and headed toward the stairs. "If anyone needs me, I'll be upstairs, playing chess with myself."

"I'm going to go change clothes, Jess," Elizabeth said as Jessica headed for the phone. "I'll be back in a minute."

Poor Jessica, Elizabeth thought as she climbed the stairs. She'd hardly spoken a word all the way home.

Elizabeth went to her bedroom and changed into a pair of jeans. She decided to wear her new blue sweatshirt with them. It was extra soft on the inside, and right now she felt like wearing something comforting and cozy. But when she looked in her bottom dresser drawer, the sweatshirt wasn't there.

That's strange, Elizabeth thought. She was sure that was where she'd put it. She searched her other drawers and her closet, with no luck. She even checked under her bed, but the sweatshirt was missing.

Missing . . . or maybe *stolen*. Elizabeth swallowed past a lump in her throat. Was it possible that her twin really was a thief?

Elizabeth looked up just as Jessica appeared in the doorway, a dejected look on her face.

"What's the verdict?" Elizabeth asked quietly.

"A few of my friends aren't sure what to believe yet—people like Mandy and Mary and Belinda. But most of them are convinced that I'm guilty." She buried her face in her hands. "You're the only one who *really* believes me, Lizzie."

Elizabeth stared at her sister sadly. "I wish I *could* really believe you, Jess."

Six

◇

Jessica's eyes went wide. "What do you mean? You don't believe me?"

Elizabeth motioned for Jessica to come in. Then she closed the door behind her. "My new blue sweatshirt is missing, Jessica."

Jessica chewed on her lower lip. "So you're saying that just because I may have borrowed your sweatshirt, that makes me the Swiper?"

"I want to believe you, I really do, but let's look at this logically. First of all, the Watchman *was* found in your locker. And everybody knows how much you wanted to borrow it."

Jessica threw her hands in the air. "Someone must have planted it there! That's the only way to explain it."

"But why? Why would anyone want to do that? And how? Your locker was locked, Jessica. And nobody knows your combination. Not even me."

Jessica lay down on Elizabeth's bed and buried her face in the pillow. "I don't know," she said in a muffled voice.

Elizabeth sighed heavily. She hated to ask her sister these questions. She probably had been interrogated enough by Mr. Clark that afternoon. But Elizabeth had to know the truth if she was going to be able to help.

"Jessica," Elizabeth said, sitting down beside her sister on the bed. "Don't you think it's an awfully strange coincidence that you've admired all the items that disappeared?"

Jessica sniffled. "Not Ellen's deodorant."

"But even that you borrow all the time."

"I like it. It smells like baby powder."

Elizabeth smiled in spite of herself. "That's not really the point. I'm trying to be logical here. And logically speaking, it's pretty strange that all the items that have vanished have been things you wanted for yourself."

"I can't help it if I'm materialistic," Jessica mumbled, still talking into her pillow. "That doesn't make me a thief."

Elizabeth frowned. "I'm sorry, I just—"

"Well, you should be sorry," Jessica said angrily, rolling onto her back. "If my own sister doesn't trust me, how can I expect anyone else to?"

"I'd probably have an easier time believing you if my clothes didn't keep disappearing."

"Those were borrowed," Jessica said, sitting up and crossing her arms over her chest. "And I wore your sweatshirt *before* you yelled at me about your sweater and *before* I promised I'd always ask first. It's probably right there in my room . . . somewhere." Jessica frowned. "I don't know why I'm even bothering to explain. It's obvious you've already made up your own mind." Her lower lip began to tremble. "But how can I get out of this if you won't help me?"

"I wish I could help," Elizabeth began. "But I don't even know where to start . . ."

"Do you know what Lila said to me on the phone?" Jessica said. "She said she was going to suggest making Veronica a Unicorn at the next meeting."

"So? I thought you were all getting along great with Veronica."

"We are. But the point is, Lila said there would probably be a vacancy in the club soon." Jessica took a shuddery breath. "A vacancy, Elizabeth! They're going to dump me from the Unicorns because they think I'm the Swiper! What ever happened to being guilty until proven innocent?"

"I think you mean that the other way around."

"Look, I know that *logically* it seems like I must be guilty," Jessica continued. She gazed at Elizabeth, her eyes bright with tears. "But sometimes you just have to believe your heart, Lizzie."

Suddenly Elizabeth made up her mind. Jessica was right. Elizabeth knew her twin better than anyone else, and her heart told her that Jessica was innocent.

"I do believe you, Jess," Elizabeth said softly.

"You do?" Jessica said hopefully, wiping away a tear.

Elizabeth nodded. "I'm not exactly sure why, to tell you the truth. But my gut instinct tells me that you didn't steal those things, despite all the evidence. For one thing, you've done lots of stupid things in your life, and you've never hesitated to confess to me before."

"Exactly!" Jessica cried.

"And the more I think about it," Elizabeth continued, "the more I wonder if the evidence against you isn't almost *too* perfect."

"Exactly!" Jessica cried again. Then she frowned. "What do you mean, *too* perfect?"

"It's something I learned from reading Amanda Howard mysteries. When a crime seems too easy to solve, there's probably a good reason."

"I don't get it," Jessica said.

"I'm not sure I do, either—yet," Elizabeth replied. "But I promise you this, Jessica. I'm going to get to the bottom of this mystery if it's the last thing I do."

"Thanks, Lizzie," Jessica said gratefully. "I knew I could count on you to get me out of this mess."

I hope you're right about that, Elizabeth thought anxiously.

"I got here as soon as I could," Amy said early that evening as Elizabeth opened the front door. "My dad drove me over. I can only stay a couple of hours, though. I hope that's enough time."

"Me, too," Elizabeth said. The more she thought about how much Jessica was depending on her, the more anxious she became.

"Where's Jessica?" Amy asked.

"In the family room, watching a game show on TV with Steven." Elizabeth shook her head. "She's really upset, Amy. She thinks the Unicorns may actually be getting ready to dump her over this."

Amy rolled her eyes. "Count on the Unicorns to overreact."

"Come on." Elizabeth motioned toward the family room. "I'll tell Jessica you're here."

Jessica and Steven were sitting on the couch, their eyes glued to the commercial playing on the TV screen.

"Hi, Amy," Jessica said sullenly. "Thanks for coming over. I can use all the help I can get."

"What are you watching?" Amy asked.

"*Q and A,*" Jessica replied. "That game show where you have to say the answers in the form of a question."

"I love this show," Amy said. "Even though I can usually only answer about two of the questions."

"Wait'll you see Steven in action," Jessica said, shaking her head. "He's gotten every one right so far. It's really weird."

"Be quiet, everyone," Steven commanded. "It'll be back on any minute."

"I heard about your genius test, Steven," Amy said. "Congratulations."

Steven waved his hand. "It's nothing I can take credit for, Amy. Just the luck of the draw. Good genes, you know."

Amy gave Jessica a doubtful look. "Is he always like this these days?"

"I'm afraid so," Jessica answered.

"Shh!" Steven hissed. "It's back."

"Watch this," Jessica whispered to Amy and Elizabeth. "You won't believe it."

One of the contestants, a petite older woman named Teresa, picked a question in the category "U.S. Geography." "And the answer is," said the announcer, " 'The state where the highest elevation in the U.S. can be found.' "

Steven frowned. "I'd have to say, 'What is Alaska?' That's where Mount McKinley is."

The announcer waited until Teresa's time had expired. "Oops, sorry, Teresa," he said brightly. "The correct question is, 'What is Alaska?' "

"See what I mean?" Jessica asked.

"I told you, dear sibling," Steven said over his shoulder. "My mind—"

"—I know," Jessica interrupted. "It's like a sponge."

"A what?" Amy asked.

"Quiet," Steven commanded. "I need to concentrate."

Teresa picked another question in the same category. "And the answer is," the announcer said, " 'The southernmost state in the United States.' "

This time Steven looked stumped. "Hmm," he murmured. "That's a toughie. But I'll say, 'What is Hawaii?' "

"No way," Jessica said. "It's obviously Florida, Steven."

"Or maybe California or Texas," Amy added.

"Nope," Steven said. "I'm pretty sure Ka Lae, Hawaii, is the southernmost place in the U.S."

Teresa guessed Florida. "Sorry, Teresa," the announcer said happily. "The correct question is, 'What is Hawaii?' Actually, the southernmost spot is called South Cape, or Ka Lae, to be exact."

Steven gave the girls a triumphant smile. For

the next few minutes, he answered every single question correctly.

"Amazing," Amy murmured. "I had no idea you were so smart, Steven."

"He's sure managed to hide it well all these years, hasn't he?" Jessica put in.

"How come you're in such a dour mood, Jessica?" Steven asked during the next commercial break.

"Translation, Lizzie?" Jessica said wearily.

"He means, why are you being so grouchy?"

"I'm *dour* because my life is pretty much over," Jessica snapped. "I've been wrongly accused of a crime."

"Several crimes, actually," Amy added.

"What kind of crime?" Steven asked.

"Some things at school have disappeared, and one of them somehow turned up in Jessica's locker," Elizabeth explained.

"Hmmm. Maybe you're a kleptomaniac," Steven suggested.

"A *what*?"

"A kleptomaniac. Someone with an uncontrollable urge to steal things."

"For your information, I did not steal anything!" Jessica exploded. She marched out of the room.

At the doorway she stopped and turned around. "Steven Wakefield, for a genius, you sure are an idiot!"

* * *

Elizabeth and Amy followed Jessica upstairs. "All right," Elizabeth said as they gathered in Jessica's bedroom, "we're going to analyze this case, just like we used to when we were Snoopers."

"Do we have to?" Jessica moaned, flopping onto the floor. "I've already been over this a million times, Elizabeth."

"Sorry, Jess," Elizabeth said. "That's how it's done."

"Pretend it's a mystery you're reading," Amy suggested as she retrieved a notepad and pen from Jessica's desk. "Have fun with it."

"Are you kidding?" Jessica cried. "Even as we speak, the rumor is being spread all over Sweet Valley that I'm a thief. By tomorrow, the entire school will have heard—"

Elizabeth cleared her throat. She was beginning to wonder if it was such a good idea to let Jessica participate. "Maybe you're too close to the case to be helpful, Jessica."

"No, please, Lizzie," Jessica pleaded. "I know I'm not as good as you and Amy are at solving mysteries, but I want to help. It's my problem, after all."

"All right, then. But no more unnecessary emotional outbursts, OK?"

Jessica pretended to zip her lips shut. "My lips are sealed," she said.

"First things first," Elizabeth said, pacing

back and forth across the floor. She always did her best thinking when she paced. "You take notes, Amy."

"Right," Amy said, nodding.

"To begin with, let's look at the facts," Elizabeth said. "All of the stolen items disappeared at school, in public places like the lunchroom, correct?"

"Of course it's correct," Jessica said impatiently. "We already *know* that, Elizabeth."

Elizabeth shot her sister a warning glance.

"Sorry."

"The question is, what does this tell us about the thief?" Elizabeth asked, clasping her hands behind her back as she paced.

"It tells us she has to be someone who blends in," Amy replied. "Someone like—" She glanced over at Jessica apologetically.

"Me," Jessica finished with a sigh.

"Fact number two," Elizabeth continued. "We know that all the items were stolen from Unicorns, except for Veronica's notebook."

"But Veronica's practically a Unicorn," Jessica said.

Elizabeth pursed her lips. "Ellen, Lila, Janet, Mandy, Veronica. All good friends of Jessica's. What does this tell us?"

"That, with the exception of Mandy, Jessica has lousy taste in friends?" Amy joked.

"Not funny, Amy," Jessica warned.

"Sorry," Amy said. "I was just trying to keep things from getting tense."

"Let's look at the stolen items," Elizabeth said. "Every one of them was an item that Jessica wanted."

"Well, the deodorant—" Jessica began.

"With the possible exception," Elizabeth added as she paced briskly toward the door, "of Ellen's deodorant—which, let's face it, no one in her right mind would want."

"Elizabeth?" Jessica asked. "Do you have to pace like that? I'm starting to get seasick."

"Sorry, Jessica." Elizabeth shook her head. "All great detectives pace. If I stop now, I may never solve your case."

Jessica sighed. "I'll close my eyes."

"We should also consider the fact that so far, only one of the stolen items has turned up," Amy pointed out. "The Watchman. And it was in Jessica's locker."

"Right," Elizabeth said. "So, putting together all the information we currently have, what does that tell us?"

For a moment, nobody spoke. "Well, it's obvious," Amy said at last, breaking the silence.

"It is?" Elizabeth asked.

Amy nodded. "Sure. Jessica did it."

Jessica groaned. "I'm doomed! I'm going to be suspended and be sent to reform school and they'll make me wear some horrible green uniform and take away my lip gloss—"

"Jessica!" Elizabeth snapped.

Jessica blinked. "Oops," she said. "Was that another unnecessary emotional outburst?"

"Sorry, Jessica," Amy said. "I shouldn't have said that. It's just that all the evidence points in your direction."

"But don't you think the evidence is a little *too* persuasive, Amy?" Elizabeth asked. "Do you know what Jessica is missing?"

"Hope," Jessica muttered.

"No." Elizabeth shook her head. "A motive."

Amy nodded. "You're right. All we have to do is figure out who *does* have one."

"You know," Elizabeth said after a few more paces, "something just occurred to me. Lila looked angry even *before* she discovered her Watchman in your locker this afternoon. It was almost as if she *expected* it to be there."

"Remember when she ran down the hall and nearly knocked us both down?" Amy asked. "I'm not sure, but I think she was carrying a piece of paper."

"A note, maybe?" Elizabeth asked hopefully.

"There's only one way to find out," Amy exclaimed. "Let's call her!"

"*I'm* not calling her," Jessica said. "Lila now officially hates me."

"Well, she's never exactly loved me," Amy

said with a wry grin. "But I'll call her." Amy headed out to the phone in the hallway.

A couple of minutes later, she burst back into the room. "Guess what? Lila said there *was* a note! She found it stuck to her locker. It said that if she ever wanted to see her Watchman again, she'd better hurry to Jessica's locker."

"Who wrote it?" Jessica demanded angrily.

"Did Lila recognize the handwriting?" Elizabeth asked.

Amy shook her head. "Whoever this person is, she's smart. The note was typed and unsigned."

"I'd like to take a look at it," Elizabeth said. "It's our only real clue."

"Unfortunately, Lila doesn't have it anymore," Amy said. "She threw it in the garbage can in the lobby."

"I'm doomed," Jessica moaned again.

"Not yet, you aren't," Elizabeth said in a determined voice. "Amy, first thing tomorrow morning, you and I are going to do a little trash excavation."

Amy made a face. "This really is beyond the call of duty, Jessica, even for a former Snooper."

Jessica flashed her a smile. "Look on the bright side, Amy. At least Lila didn't throw the note away in the lunchroom trash can."

"Let's keep our fingers crossed," Elizabeth said. "Right now, that note is our only hope."

Seven

◇

"I sure hope Jessica appreciates this," Amy muttered as she dug through the large trash barrel in the school lobby the next morning. She and Elizabeth had arrived forty-five minutes before homeroom, and the school was nearly deserted.

"Jessica was going to help," Elizabeth said as she stretched her arm deep into the barrel. "But I think she's really dreading coming to school today and facing everyone. The last thing she wanted to do was get here early and be seen digging through the trash for Lila's note. Besides, she really isn't a lot of help, you have to admit. She's too emotional right now."

Amy frowned. "Well, I'm going to get pretty emotional too, if I have to bury my head in this trash can much longer." She glanced over her shoulder. "Hardly anyone's here yet. Why don't we save time and just dump this on the floor and dig through it? It's mostly paper, anyway."

"I'm game if you are."

The two girls turned the barrel over and shook it, spreading a huge mound of trash on the lobby floor. "Talk about a needle in a haystack," Elizabeth said with a sigh.

"Well, we know the note's on plain paper, and that it was typed," Amy said as she began to sift through the mess. "That should help us narrow things down."

Suddenly they heard the steady tap of footsteps coming down the hallway. "It's the Hairnet!" Amy whispered, glancing over her shoulder.

"Girls?" Mrs. Arnette called. "What on earth are you doing?"

"It's . . . it's a recycling project for science, Mrs. Arnette," Elizabeth said. "We're analyzing the nature of the trash the school generates."

"We'll be coming by to study your trash soon," Amy added.

"Well, I suppose if it's for a good cause," Mrs. Arnette said doubtfully.

"Oh, it's *definitely* for a good cause," Elizabeth said.

Mrs. Arnette walked away, shaking her head.

"That was close," Elizabeth whispered as she

continued digging. "We'd better hurry before more people start showing up." When Amy didn't answer, Elizabeth looked over. Amy was studying a piece of wrinkled paper intently. "Amy!" she exclaimed. "Did you find it?"

"What?" Amy asked, looking up. "Oh, sorry. This is a page from somebody's book report. It really sounds like a great book. Listen—"

"Amy!" Elizabeth cried. "We're not here to read the trash."

"Sorry," Amy said. She folded up the paper and stuck it in her pocket.

For the next few minutes, the girls worked in silence. Finally Elizabeth leaned back and sighed. "It's no use," she said wearily.

"Do you think Lila could have been wrong about the trash can she used?" Amy asked as she began shoveling paper back into the can.

"This is the only can here, and she did say the lobby, right?"

Amy nodded. "Of course, there's that little can around the corner by the drinking fountain. That's practically in the lobby."

Elizabeth dumped a last armful of trash into the barrel. "It's worth a try. Besides, we're getting pretty good at this."

The girls headed for the small trash can in the hallway nearby. "Empty!" Elizabeth exclaimed unhappily.

"Looking for something, young lady?"

Elizabeth turned to see Mr. Jansen, one of the school custodians. "I know this sounds crazy," she said, "but do you know where this trash went? We're looking for a very important piece of paper."

Mr. Jansen shook his head. "That was emptied yesterday afternoon, I'm afraid. Chances are, whatever you're looking for is out in the dumpster behind the school by now."

Elizabeth looked at Amy hopefully.

"No way," Amy said. "I am not digging through that dumpster, even if it means saving your sister's neck."

"Whatever you're looking for would probably be near the top," Mr. Jansen said. "Course I can't guarantee anything."

"Thanks, Mr. Jansen." Elizabeth turned to Amy. "You don't have to come," she said, squaring her shoulders. "But I'm going to check it out."

"Elizabeth," Amy said tolerantly, "not even Amanda Howard would go this far. But if you're going, I'm going. It's a dirty job, but somebody's got to do it." She smiled. "And by the way, it's mostly going to be you!"

They headed outside into the bright morning sunshine. As they approached the large green dumpster behind the school, Amy pinched her nose. "Phew! Are you sure you want to go through with this?"

Elizabeth made a face. "What *is* that smell, do you think?"

"Let's see. What were they serving for lunch yesterday?"

"Goulash."

"That explains it."

Standing on tiptoes, the girls could just reach the top layer of garbage. They rolled up their sleeves and began picking through it carefully. But after a few minutes, even Elizabeth could see it was a hopeless task. There was too much garbage, and they had too little time. They were never going to find the clue they needed.

"OK, Amy," she said at last, "I'm ready to admit defeat. Let's go wash up."

Amy leaned toward Elizabeth and sniffed. "Speaking of washing up, I've been meaning to ask you. What is that lovely fragrance you're wearing today?"

"Do you really like it?" Elizabeth asked with a grin. "It's called *Goulash Memories.*"

"Are you sure the Unicorns don't want you to sit with them, Jess?" Elizabeth asked as Jessica sat down next to Amy at lunch.

"Hey, I can take a hint," Jessica said. "Lila refuses to talk to me, Veronica's been giving me these snide smiles all morning, and everybody else has been whispering about me behind my back." She took a deep breath. "And that's just what I've had to put up with this morning! I can't wait to see what the rest of the day will bring."

"Give it a day or two," Elizabeth advised. "It'll blow over."

"Lizzie," Jessica said, "you're such an optimist. Nothing's going to blow over. In fact, it's going to get a whole lot worse when I find out what Mr. Clark's going to do to me." She opened her milk and stared at it dejectedly. "Do you really think he'll suspend me?"

"Mr. Clark is usually pretty fair," Amy said.

"Jessica," Elizabeth whispered. "Don't look now, but Ellen's heading this way."

"See?" Amy said. "Who says the Unicorns aren't speaking to you?"

Jessica looked up hopefully as Ellen marched over to the table.

"Jessica," Ellen began, "I know how everyone else is treating you, and I have to say, I don't think it's right."

Jessica's face melted into a smile. "Finally!" she cried in a relieved voice.

"We should do more than just avoid you," Ellen continued. "I say we should make you *pay* for what you've done." She dropped a piece of paper on the table in front of Jessica.

"What's this?" Jessica asked suspiciously.

"A bill," Ellen replied. "For the cost of my mother's earrings. Plus ten extra dollars, for pain and suffering."

"Pain and suffering?" Jessica shrieked. Several people at nearby tables turned to stare.

"I *was* grounded for an entire week," Ellen reminded her.

Jessica crumpled the paper into a ball. "That's what I think of your bill, Ellen," she yelled. "Now, do you want to hear what I think of *you*?"

Ellen took a step backward. "I want those earrings back," she said nervously.

"Well, you're asking the wrong person for them," Jessica cried. "Now get lost, Ellen!"

Jessica's voice seemed to echo through the cafeteria for a moment. Then the people at nearby tables started whispering and giggling. Jessica glanced over at the Unicorner and saw Ellen sit down and begin whispering to Lila. Both girls shot Jessica an angry look.

"I have never been so humiliated in my entire life," Jessica moaned.

"Uh-oh," Amy whispered to Elizabeth, nodding her head toward the aisle, where Aaron Dallas was approaching.

"Now what?" Jessica asked.

"Aaron's coming," Elizabeth said softly.

"Is it too late to crawl under the table?" Jessica whispered.

"Hey, Jessica," Aaron said, pausing next to Jessica's chair.

"Look, Aaron, I just want to say that whatever you've heard, don't believe it—" Jessica began.

"You mean that Swiper stuff?" Aaron said with a shrug. "Hey, I know you didn't do it."

"You do?" Jessica said gratefully.

"Sure." Aaron cleared his throat and gestured toward a table a few rows away. "Since you're not sitting with the Unicorns, I was wondering—" He paused, looking a little hesitant, "if you would maybe want to sit with me today?"

Jessica cast a hopeful look at Elizabeth. "Do you mind?"

"Of course not," Elizabeth assured her.

"Good," Jessica said, rising. "Because the truth is, you both smell a little funny!"

"The earliest form of turtles appeared during the Paleozoic Era, which of course preceded the Mesozoic Era," Steven said at dinner that evening as he reached for the salad bowl.

"Of course," Joe Howell said with a sigh.

Mr. and Mrs. Wakefield nodded wearily.

"Which of course preceded the Cenozoic Era, my personal favorite of the geological periods," Steven continued.

"Let me get this right," Joe said. "You have a *favorite* geological period?"

"Sure," Steven replied. "Don't you?"

Elizabeth rolled her eyes at Jessica, but Jessica was staring into space.

When Steven finally interrupted his monologue to eat his salad, Jessica spoke up. "Dad," she said, "what does a judge do to a person accused of stealing things?"

"That depends," Mr. Wakefield replied. "Sometimes, if it's a first offense, he or she has the guilty person do community service. Sometimes, the person goes to jail."

Jessica gulped. "What if the person keeps stealing stuff, over and over?"

"That would be a repeat offender," Mr. Wakefield replied. "Judges tend to deal more harshly with them."

"Oh," Jessica said in a tiny voice.

"You didn't really turn out to be a kleptomaniac, did you?" Steven asked, sounding almost like his old self for a moment.

"Steven!" Mrs. Wakefield exclaimed. "What are you talking about?"

"Jessica," Steven said with a shrug. "She's a klepto."

"She is not," Elizabeth interjected. "Everyone just *thinks* she is."

Jessica shot Elizabeth a desperate look.

Mr. Wakefield threw up his hands in exasperation. "Why do I have the feeling I'm missing something here?" he asked.

Elizabeth sighed. "We think someone is framing Jessica to look like the Sweet Valley Swiper,

Dad," Elizabeth explained. "One of the stolen items was found in her locker."

"Honey," Mrs. Wakefield exclaimed, "is this true?"

"Yes," Jessica said dejectedly. "And I'll understand if you don't believe me. Just promise you'll come visit me in reform school, OK? I'm sure they have visiting hours."

"No one is going to reform school," Mr. Wakefield said calmly. "I'm going to call your principal first thing Monday morning, and I'm sure we'll get this whole thing straightened out."

"We've been trying to find some evidence to prove that Jessica's innocent," Elizabeth said. "But so far, we've come up empty-handed."

"Sweetheart, you should have come to us right away with something this important," Mrs. Wakefield said to Jessica.

"What's the point?" Jessica muttered. "Everybody already thinks I'm guilty."

"Besides, Amy and I thought we could solve the crime on our own and save Jessica," Elizabeth admitted quietly.

"Elizabeth, this isn't some Amanda Howard mystery," Mr. Wakefield said. "I know you're just trying to help, but Jessica could be in very serious trouble. Haven't we already been through this with the last mystery you tried to solve? The charm school?"

Elizabeth stared at her plate. Her father was

right. This wasn't a game. "I'm sorry, Dad. I guess I was hoping I could save the day."

"That's okay, Lizzie," Jessica said. "It's not your fault. I was hoping you could, too."

"I'm sorry I got you in hot water like that, Jess," Elizabeth said unhappily as the twins headed upstairs after dinner.

"That's OK," Jessica reassured her. "They were going to find out sooner or later. I'd rather they hear about it from you and me than from Mr. Clark."

Suddenly Elizabeth stopped. "Did you hear that?"

Jessica frowned. "It sounds like Steven and Joe are arguing. Come on." She nodded toward Steven's door. "What are you waiting for? You're the Snooper. So let's snoop."

The girls tiptoed down the hallway and positioned themselves on either side of Steven's bedroom door.

"Steven, you've got to be kidding," they heard Joe say in a loud, very frustrated voice.

"Kidding?" Steven echoed.

"This time you've gone too far!" Joe cried. "I mean, what happened to the old Steven? The one who used to be fun to hang out with?"

Steven laughed. "That Steven was an intellectual lightweight, dear friend."

"And stop calling me *dear friend!*" Joe shouted.

Both girls covered their mouths to keep from laughing.

"Why can't we call Cathy and Jenna?" Joe whined. "We could go to a movie. *Alien Invasion, Part Four* is playing at the Sweet Valley Cinema."

"Cathy's baby-sitting tonight," Steven replied. "Besides, you're going to like this even better than *Alien Invasion*, part whatever."

Suddenly the door swung open and both girls jumped. Jessica dashed for the telephone and pretended to be dialing a number.

Steven didn't even seem to notice the twins. He headed toward the stairs, with Joe trailing miserably behind. "Trust me, Joe," Steven said. "You'll be grateful I taped this for you. And the wonderful thing is, it's three hours long, with no commercial breaks."

"Where are you going?" Elizabeth asked Joe as he cast her a plaintive look.

"Where else?" Joe asked. "To watch *Porcupine Love—the Untold Story*."

"I'm glad you talked me into coming to the mall today," Jessica said. It was Saturday afternoon, and she was sitting with Elizabeth and Amy at a table in the food court, watching the crowd and eating frozen yogurt. "You guys aren't nearly as much fun to shop with as the Unicorns, but you'll do."

"Gee, thanks, Jessica," Amy said with a wry grin.

Elizabeth smiled. She was glad she'd convinced Jessica to get out of the house for a while. Jessica seemed to have forgotten all about the whole Swiper thing for the moment. The only problem was that Elizabeth herself couldn't seem to stop thinking about it.

"What are you thinking, Elizabeth?" Amy prodded a few minutes later. "You're being so quiet."

Elizabeth took another spoonful of yogurt. "Nothing, really."

"I know," Jessica said. "She's still trying to figure out the Swiper case, aren't you, Elizabeth?"

"I know it's crazy, but I just can't seem to let it go," Elizabeth admitted.

"This is one whodunit I'm afraid we're not going to solve," Amy said.

"The same question keeps running through my mind, over and over again," Elizabeth said. "Obviously, someone is trying to make Jessica's best friends hate her. But what would anyone have to gain from that?"

"Maybe someone's mad at me for something I don't even remember doing," Jessica said resignedly. "Or maybe they're jealous."

Just then Elizabeth looked across the food court and noticed several of the Unicorns walking out of Kendall's, a large department store.

"Jess," Elizabeth said quietly. "Don't look now, but there are some Unicorns over there, behind you."

Amy twisted around to look, while Jessica ducked her head. "How many?" Jessica whispered.

"A whole herd," Amy said. "Lila, Ellen, Janet, Kimberly, Mandy, Belinda, and Veronica."

"Veronica's not really a Unicorn," Jessica corrected. Then she sighed. "But she might as well be."

"Good news," Amy said. "It looks like they're leaving."

"That's a relief," Jessica said. "I couldn't bear the humiliation of being caught here with—" Suddenly she stopped and gave a sheepish grin. "I didn't mean it that way. I just—Elizabeth? Really, I didn't mean to hurt your feelings—"

Elizabeth didn't answer.

"Lizzie?" Jessica prompted anxiously. "You're not mad, are you?"

"You bet I'm mad," Elizabeth exclaimed. "But not at you, Jessica."

Jessica exchanged a confused glance with Amy. "What are you talking about?" Jessica asked.

"I think I may finally be onto something," Elizabeth murmured.

"You mean you've solved the Swiper mystery?" Jessica cried.

"Maybe so," Elizabeth said slowly. "But it's not going to be easy to prove."

Eight

"OK," Elizabeth said nervously on Monday morning. "Let's go over our plan one more time."

Jessica giggled. She was sitting in her bed, still wearing her pajamas. "We spent all day yesterday planning, Elizabeth. Don't you think we're organized enough?"

"Let's just say I'd feel better if we went through it again. Now, do you have the heating pad plugged in?"

"Check," Jessica said.

"And you already ran the thermometer under hot water?"

"Check," Jessica said. "Right now it reads one hundred and seven degrees."

"One hundred and seven!" Elizabeth cried.

"Jessica, you'd be delirious with a temperature that high. Don't you think you're getting carried away?"

"You said we wanted to be convincing. And you know Mom—she knows all my tricks. She's going to be especially suspicious since she knows I don't want to go to school and face everyone again."

"Well, you're a great actress," Elizabeth reminded her twin as she picked up her backpack. "You can do it." She crossed her fingers. "I just hope I can."

"Wait," Jessica said. "Let me see what you're bringing to wear."

Elizabeth pulled out a rolled-up purple miniskirt and a matching top.

"Perfect," Jessica said approvingly.

"It sure feels good to be stealing some of *your* clothes for a change!"

"Did you remember to bring some of my lip gloss?" Jessica asked.

Elizabeth nodded. "I even have some gum to chew during homeroom to annoy Mr. Davis."

"You do know me well," Jessica said with a laugh. "Don't forget to take your barrette out, too."

Elizabeth glanced at the door. "I hear Mom," she whispered. "Quick! The heating pad!"

Jessica reached under the covers for the heating pad. She held it against her cheeks until they turned warm and pink.

"Jessica?" Mrs. Wakefield said, peeking into the room just as Jessica shoved the heating pad back under the covers. "What are you still doing in bed?"

"She doesn't look so great, Mom," Elizabeth said.

"Ohh," Jessica moaned. "I think I have something awful, Mom. I may even be delirious."

Elizabeth rolled her eyes. Count on Jessica to ham it up!

"Delirious, huh?" Mrs. Wakefield said skeptically, stepping into the room. She reached over to feel Jessica's head. While her mother's back was turned, Elizabeth quickly shoved Jessica's clothes back into her backpack.

"Well, you do feel hot," Mrs. Wakefield said. "I don't suppose that's artificial heat I'm feeling?"

"Artificial?" Jessica moaned, managing a pathetic cough.

"Caused by a hot towel, say, or maybe the heating pad?"

Jessica tried another feeble cough and gave Elizabeth a desperate look.

"I'll get the thermometer, Mom," Elizabeth said. She went into the bathroom and grabbed the thermometer. Then she rushed back out and stuck it in her sister's mouth. Elizabeth hated to trick her mother this way, but she reminded herself it *was* for a good cause.

"She doesn't look good to me," Elizabeth said, shaking her head.

Mrs. Wakefield waited for a few minutes, then removed the thermometer. "One hundred and six," she read. She smiled. "No wonder you're delirious, Jessica."

Jessica closed her eyes. "Mom?" she groaned. "Is that you I hear?"

"Look, honey," Mrs. Wakefield said gently. "I don't blame you for not wanting to go to school today. But you're going to have to face your problems eventually. Dad said he'd call Mr. Clark this afternoon—"

"Ohh," Jessica moaned, clutching at her stomach.

Mrs. Wakefield put her hands on her hips. "Look, if you're not feeling well enough to go to school today," she said, "then you're not feeling well enough to move from this bed, understand? No soap operas, no nothing."

Jessica nodded. "Maybe I could watch *Days of Turmoil* this afternoon, if I start feeling better," she added meekly.

"We wouldn't want you to strain yourself, now would we?" Mrs. Wakefield asked. "Besides, honey, you probably wouldn't be able to follow the plot—what with being delirious and all."

"Well, I'd better get going," Elizabeth said

quickly. "I wouldn't want to catch whatever it is that Jessica has."

"I suspect that what she really has is a serious case of bad acting," Mrs. Wakefield said.

"Good luck, Lizzie," Jessica said with another moan.

"Good luck?" Mrs. Wakefield echoed. "For what?" She cast Jessica a doubtful look. "Don't tell me you have a test today—"

"No!" Jessica exclaimed. "I promise! I didn't really mean good luck. I meant good-bye." She clapped her hand to her forehead. "It's the fever, Mom. I don't know what I'm saying."

"Hope you're better soon," Elizabeth called as she sailed out the door. *Phase one accomplished*, she told herself. But that was the easy part. Now it was Elizabeth's turn to act.

"How did it go?" Amy asked Elizabeth when they met in the girls' bathroom before homeroom.

"Jessica overacted a little, but my mom let her stay home anyway," Elizabeth said.

"So far, so good," Amy whispered.

Elizabeth glanced over her shoulder. "This would probably be as good a time as any for Phase Two," she said under her breath. "There's just that one eighth grader over there."

Amy nodded. "The bathroom probably won't get any emptier."

Elizabeth headed for the last stall. "I'm going in as Elizabeth, but I'm coming out as Jessica."

"Just like Clark Kent going into a phone booth and coming out as Superman," Amy said. "It's a bird! It's a plane! It's Supertwin!"

Elizabeth quickly changed into Jessica's skirt and top and removed her barrette so her hair hung in long, loose waves around her face. As she slicked on a little lip gloss, she heard Amy's voice. "Hi, *Lila*," Amy practically shouted. "What's new?"

Thanks, Amy, Elizabeth thought to herself. She stepped out of the stall, wondering what to say to Lila. Were Lila and Jessica even speaking?

She stepped over to one of the sinks and began washing her hands. Lila took one look at her and tilted her nose in the air. "Excuse me," she said, pushing Elizabeth aside as she marched out the door. "I don't want to breathe the same air as a *criminal*."

"I am *not* a criminal," Elizabeth cried in a wounded voice, doing her best to sound like Jessica.

As Lila disappeared out the door, Elizabeth breathed a sigh of relief. Lila was Jessica's closest friend. If she believed Elizabeth was Jessica, everyone would.

"Nice job," Amy whispered, rushing to Elizabeth's side. "You almost had me convinced."

As Elizabeth grinned at her reflection in the

mirror, she noticed the eighth grader standing behind her, staring and shaking her head. "I could have sworn you were wearing a blue dress a minute ago," the girl said.

"Nope," Elizabeth said. "Your eyes must be playing tricks on you. Are you feeling OK?"

During homeroom, Elizabeth made sure to snap her gum extra loudly while Mr. Davis called the roll. When he got to her own name, she raised her hand. "Elizabeth's sick today," she said. "I think she has the flu."

"Thank you, Jessica," Mr. Davis said. "And by the way, may I ask where the gum came from?"

"She probably stole it," Lila called out.

There was a chorus of laughter, as Mr. Davis sent Lila a warning look. "That's enough, Lila. Jessica, if you don't get rid of that gum in the next five seconds, I'm going to write you up a nice detention slip."

Elizabeth quickly swallowed her gum. This wasn't the first time she'd pretended to be her twin, but it never failed to amaze her how dangerous being Jessica could be.

When homeroom ended, Elizabeth put Phase Three into action. She watched as Veronica stood and picked up her books, then raced to catch up with her as she made her way into the hall.

"Hi, Veronica," she said cheerfully, falling into step beside her.

Veronica looked at her doubtfully, as if she wasn't quite sure she wanted to be seen with her.

"Can you believe Mr. Davis and his gum hangup?" Elizabeth asked with a laugh. "He's got to be the only teacher in the school who'd give you a detention for blowing a few bubbles during class."

Veronica stopped and gazed at Jessica with an expression that was a mixture of annoyance and doubt. "How come you're in such a good mood, Jessica?" she demanded. "Everyone's furious at you."

"Well, I guess it's true that most of the Unicorns are a little mad at me," Elizabeth admitted.

"A little mad? They hate your guts!"

Elizabeth shrugged. "I still have Mandy on my side, at least."

"What do you mean?" Veronica asked, frowning.

"She and I had a long talk," Elizabeth replied. "And she's not mad at me anymore. After all, she just lost a couple of thrift-store things." Elizabeth leaned closer. "The only thing in the world that would *really* upset Mandy," she said, her voice lowered, "would be if she lost her rhinestone heart pin. You know the one she always wears?"

Veronica nodded thoughtfully. "Sure," she said slowly. "It's a great pin."

"So anyway," Elizabeth continued, "why should I be in a bad mood? As long as I have Mandy on my side, the rest of the Unicorns will come around eventually. This is all bound to blow over."

"I really hope so," Veronica said with a slight smile, "for your sake, Jessica."

"Well, I gotta run," Elizabeth said brightly. "I can't afford to be late this week. I'm already in enough trouble."

She walked off and caught up with Amy around the corner. "How did it go?" Amy whispered.

"She took the bait," Elizabeth replied, crossing her fingers. "Now we'll see if we can reel her in."

Elizabeth had just finished lunch and was walking down the hall toward her locker when she heard rapid footsteps behind her. "Here comes Phase Four," she murmured under her breath. "I hope."

"Jessica Wakefield!" Mandy screamed. "Stop!"

Elizabeth stopped in midstride and spun around. Mandy and Lila were dashing toward her with angry, determined looks on their faces.

"How could you?" Mandy cried, waving a piece of paper in Elizabeth's face.

"You snake!" Lila yelled. "It was rotten

enough for you to steal my Watchman. But Mandy's pin, Jessica? I mean, I'm rich. I can replace the stuff you stole. But Mandy's poor—"

"Thanks, Lila," Mandy said, rolling her eyes. "But I can take care of myself." She pointed to the paper she was holding. "I want to see inside your locker this instant, Jessica. This letter says you stole my pin, and I'm betting that's where I'll find it."

"Just like my Watchman," Lila added.

Elizabeth smiled in spite of herself.

"You think this is funny?" Lila cried. "You won't be laughing when we tell Mr. Clark about this!"

Mandy heaved a sigh. "I thought we were friends, Jessica. I can't believe you'd do this."

"Mandy," Elizabeth said softly, "I'm not Jessica."

"Who are you, then?" Lila demanded. "Robin Hood?"

"I'm Elizabeth."

"Cut it out, Jessica," Lila scoffed. "That's truly pathetic, trying to pretend you're Elizabeth so you can blame it on her."

"No, really!" Elizabeth cried. Somehow she hadn't bargained on this response. She'd just assumed Mandy and Lila would believe her.

Just then, to Elizabeth's relief, Amy stepped forward. "That's Elizabeth, you guys. I guarantee it."

Lila and Mandy exchanged doubtful glances. "Jessica's home sick," Elizabeth said. "Call my house and see."

Mandy shook her head. "This whole thing is getting way too weird."

"Here." Amy dug in her pocket and pulled out a quarter. "Call. It's the only way you'll be sure."

"This is ridiculous, Jessica," Lila fumed.

"Come on, Lila," Mandy said. "It can't hurt to call and see. I'll do anything to get my pin back."

Mandy led the way to the pay phone in the lobby. "Here goes nothing," she said as she dialed the Wakefields' number.

While the phone rang, Lila tapped her foot impatiently. "I know it's you, Jessica," she said, glaring at Elizabeth.

"How?" Elizabeth asked, smiling.

"I can tell from the sneaky expression on your face."

"Shh," Mandy hissed. "Hello? Mrs. Wakefield?" she said into the receiver. "Um, this may sound crazy, but is Jessica there?"

A second later her eyes widened. "Really?" She put her hand over the receiver. "She says Jessica's home, sort-of sick. She's getting her to come to the phone."

"See?" Elizabeth said triumphantly.

Lila frowned. "How do we know that isn't

Elizabeth at home, fooling Mrs. Wakefield into thinking she's Jessica?"

"Oh, please, Lila!" Amy groaned.

"No," Mandy said. "Lila has a point. When whoever this is at home gets on the line, I'm going to give her a little quiz. It's the only way to find out for sure."

"Phase Four is getting a little messy," Elizabeth whispered to Amy.

"Hello, Jessica?" Mandy said. "How do I know this is really you?" She listened for a moment. "Well, she *says* she's Elizabeth, but Lila and I still have our doubts. Hold on a minute, will you?"

Mandy covered the receiver. "Quick," she said to Elizabeth, "Jess—I mean, Eliza—*whoever* you are! Tell me the first name of Jake Sommers's fiancée."

Elizabeth threw up her hands. "How should I know?"

Mandy frowned. "That's a good start," she said to Lila. "Elizabeth wouldn't have a clue." Suddenly Mandy's eyes narrowed. "Of course," she said to Elizabeth, "you could still be Jessica, cleverly pretending not to have a clue."

"She *is* a sneaky criminal," Lila pointed out.

Mandy put the phone to her ear. "Whoever you are, there at the Wakefields' house. Can you tell me the first name of Jake Sommers's fiancée?"

Mandy paused, then nodded. "She knew it was Shelby," she said to Lila. "Now what?"

Lila pursed her lips. "Suppose we reverse it, just to be sure. Ask the phone twin something only Elizabeth would know."

Mandy scratched her head. "Hello, phone twin?" she said after a few seconds. "Can you spell *thief* for me?"

Suddenly Mandy laughed. "T-H-E-I-F? Don't you remember the rule that says *I before E, except after C,* Jessica?" Mandy rolled her eyes at Lila. "Trust me. This is *definitely* Jessica I'm talking to. She's always been a lousy speller."

"But what about the note?" Lila asked. "This doesn't make any sense."

"Jessica?" Mandy said into the phone. "We've got a very confusing situation on our hands here. Do you think you could give us your locker combination? Lila and I need to check something."

"We sure do," Lila muttered, still looking suspicious.

"OK," Mandy said when she hung up. "Remember this. 32-3-16. Now let's go check Jessica's locker."

"I just don't get it," Lila said as the four girls marched down the hallway. "If you're really Elizabeth, and Jessica is really at home, then why did Mandy find this note in her notebook about her pin? I mean, Mandy's pin really *is* missing."

They reached Jessica's locker and Mandy began to turn the lock.

"There's a very logical explanation," Elizabeth began, but before she could continue, Mandy opened the door and gasped.

"My pin!" she cried. "It really *is* here!" She grabbed it and turned to face Elizabeth. "This would be a great time to hear that logical explanation, Elizabeth. If Jessica's not guilty, then who put this pin in her locker?"

Nine

◇

Elizabeth took a deep breath. "This morning I had a little talk with Veronica," she explained to Lila and Mandy. "I told her that nothing would upset Mandy more than having her rhinestone pin stolen." She smiled. "Of course, Veronica *thought* she was talking to Jessica."

"Veronica?" Mandy said in disbelief. "Are you saying that you think she's the real Swiper?"

"She's been so nice to the Unicorns," Lila protested. "Why would she steal our stuff?"

"The more important question is, why she would want to make it look like Jessica stole your stuff?" Amy said.

"Amy and I think that Veronica's been trying

to get Jessica out of the picture so she can take her place in the Unicorns," Elizabeth explained.

"Speak of the devil," Mandy whispered. "Look who's coming."

Elizabeth glanced around and saw that Veronica was strolling down the hall, heading straight for them. Elizabeth kicked Jessica's locker shut with her foot and turned to Amy. "Time for Phase Five," she whispered. "Go get Mr. Clark, quick."

As Amy dashed off, Elizabeth turned back to Mandy and Lila. "Have you told anyone about the missing pin yet?"

"No one yet," Mandy said. "We just found the note."

"Great," Elizabeth whispered. "When Veronica gets here, I'm Jessica, and you're furious, OK? Don't say too much," she added. "Let Veronica do all the talking."

"I don't get it," Lila said, frowning.

"That's OK," Mandy said, smiling at Elizabeth. "I think I do."

As Veronica approached, Elizabeth took a deep breath. This was her chance to solve the Swiper mystery, once and for all. And it might be her only opportunity to clear Jessica's name. She crossed her fingers. "What are you talking about, Mandy?" she exclaimed loudly.

Mandy frowned menacingly. "How could you do this to me, Jessica?" she cried. "You know how much it meant to me!"

"Really, Jessica," Lila spoke up, although she didn't look quite sure that she knew what she was talking about.

"I thought you were my friend, Jessica," Mandy moaned as Veronica sidled up alongside Lila, watching the whole scene curiously. "You could have taken anything, anything but that."

"It had so much sentimental value," Lila added.

"You know how much that pin meant to Mandy," Veronica chimed in.

Suddenly everyone fell silent. All eyes were on Veronica.

"What pin?" Mandy asked.

"Your rhinestone pin, of course," Veronica replied.

Elizabeth took a step forward. "What makes you think Mandy lost it, Veronica?"

Veronica cleared her throat. "Um . . . Janet told me," she said after a moment's hesitation.

Mandy crossed her arms over her chest. "But I didn't tell Janet about it."

"Maybe someone else told Janet you couldn't find it," Veronica said quickly, her eyes darting up and down the hallway.

"That's impossible," Mandy said softly. "Because I didn't lose it."

"You did so!" Veronica cried.

Elizabeth gave Mandy a grim smile. "How

would you know, Veronica?" she asked. "Unless you took it yourself."

"Look, Jessica," Veronica growled. "Don't try to blame me for what you did."

"I'm not Jessica. I'm Elizabeth," Elizabeth said calmly. "And Jessica didn't do anything, because she's not even at school today. We know you did it, Veronica."

For a moment Veronica seemed to panic, but suddenly she smiled. "I'd love to see you try to prove that," she said coolly, crossing her arms over her chest.

"I think I'll try," said a man's voice.

Elizabeth spun around to see Mr. Clark approaching with Amy. "I told him the whole story," Amy said breathlessly.

"Veronica," Mr. Clark said. "I'd like to have a look in your locker, please."

"No!" Veronica cried angrily. "I don't have to show you anything! I'll—I'll call my parents, and they'll call a lawyer, and . . ." Her voice trailed off.

"Come on, Veronica," Mr. Clark said seriously. "Let's get this over with."

At last Veronica relented. She trudged down to her locker and slowly opened the lock.

"I believe this is one of the items reported stolen, isn't it?" Mr. Clark said, pulling out a wide-brimmed hat.

"My hat," Mandy cried. She peered over Mr. Clark's shoulder. "And my jean jacket!"

"And there's my magazine," Lila exclaimed. She turned on Veronica. "I can't believe it was you, all along!"

Veronica stared at the floor, her face frozen in a frown.

"How could we have been so wrong about you?" Mandy said, staring at Veronica.

"And so wrong about Jessica?" Lila added quietly.

"Elizabeth, you're the best sister in the whole world," Jessica exclaimed when Elizabeth called to tell her the news. "I knew you could do it."

"You did?" Elizabeth asked with a laugh. "That's not quite how I remember it."

"Oh, I always had faith in you," Jessica assured her. "Just like you did in me. What are sisters for, after all?"

When Jessica hung up the phone, she ran to tell Mrs. Wakefield the wonderful news. "I'm so relieved for you, honey," Mrs. Wakefield said. "Let's celebrate with some chocolate-chip cookies."

"I guess it's too late for me to go back to school today," Jessica said. "But now that I'm feeling so much better—" she gave her mother a sly glance—"I suppose it wouldn't hurt for me to catch up on *Days of Turmoil*."

Mrs. Wakefield laughed. "Tell you what. I'll make a deal with you. I'll even watch *Days of Turmoil* with you, if you'll give me a hand straightening up the house afterward."

"Deal," Jessica said. "I'm in such a good mood, I'll do the whole upstairs myself!"

It was an especially touching *Days of Turmoil*. Jake Sommers's character, Lance, was jilted at the altar, right before he was about to marry his long-lost ex-girlfriend, who'd run away with the circus when she got amnesia and fell for a fire-eater. Jessica used up several tissues, sniffling.

She was still thinking about Jake when she went upstairs to vacuum and dust. Shelby was so lucky! Marrying Jake would be like a dream come true. Sure, there'd be boring parts, like the household chores, but there was no reason Jake couldn't help. Jessica was sure that he was a liberated guy.

Jessica steered the vacuum into Steven's room. Normally, that would have been tricky, since Steven stored most of his clothes on the floor, just like Jessica did. But ever since his personality transformation, he'd gotten much neater.

Jessica picked up one of Steven's CDs off the floor. "Wagner's Greatest Hits," she read. She turned the CD over, and was surprised to see a label from the Sweet Valley Public Library. She frowned. Hadn't Steven said he'd *bought* his new opera CD?

With a shrug, she went back to work and

poked the vacuum under the bed. Suddenly it made a loud noise. "Great," Jessica murmured, "what did you eat now?"

She unplugged the vacuum, turned it over, and got down on her hands and knees to inspect the bottom. Sure enough, poking out between the brushes was one of Steven's gym socks. Jessica yanked it loose. *I'd better check to see if the other one's under there*, she thought.

As she searched under Steven's bed, her hand landed on a crumpled piece of paper. Curious, she pulled it out and unfolded it. Scribbled on the sheet in Steven's nearly illegible handwriting was a list of questions: *What is the Statue of Liberty? What is an aardvark? What is Alaska? What is Hawaii?*

Suddenly Jessica gasped. These were the same answers Steven had known when they'd watched *Q and A* the other night! What was going on?

And then it hit her. *Steven had cheated!* Somehow, he'd memorized the answers to the show, just to make everyone believe he really knew them. But why? If Steven was so intelligent, why would he resort to a cheat sheet? Unless—

Jessica stood up and gazed around the room. She was about to do a little snooping of her own.

Steven got home before Elizabeth did. When he came through the front door, Jessica was waiting for him in the family room. "Hello, dear sibling," she called.

Steven dropped his books on the couch. "Hello," he said, eyeing her doubtfully. "How come you're home so early?"

"I stayed home from school. I was sick."

"Ah," Steven said knowingly. "The Swiper thing was getting to you, no doubt."

"Actually, Elizabeth figured out the mystery today and cleared my name."

"That's good news," Steven said as he flopped into a chair. "I never really thought you were a kleptomaniac, you know."

"That's OK," Jessica said with a grin. "I never really thought you were a genius."

Steven gave Jessica a sidelong glance. "Jessica, you're such a kidder," he said, sounding a bit uncertain. He reached for the remote control. "Perhaps there's something on educational TV we could enjoy together."

"Try Sesame Street on channel two," Jessica suggested.

"Look, Jessica, I know it's difficult adjusting to my new intellectual status—"

"—or better yet," Jessica interrupted, "let's see what's on tape."

Steven frowned. "Why? Did you tape something?"

"No. You did. Push the play button, dear sib."

Steven pushed the button and the screen flickered to life. "And the answer is," said the *Q and A* announcer, " 'The state where the highest elevation in the U.S. can be found.' "

Steven cleared his throat. "I wonder how this got taped?" he asked. "Perhaps I inadvertently pushed the record button during the show."

"Or perhaps you taped the show, then ran it for Elizabeth and me, pretending it was new."

"That's crazy, Jessica."

"Crazy, yes. But true."

Steven scowled. "In the first place, why would I pull such a juvenile trick?"

"So you could memorize the answers and make yourself look brilliant."

"Even if I *had* done something that dumb," Steven continued, "you or Elizabeth would have noticed the play button glowing on the VCR, don't you think?"

"That's why you put this black tape over the button," Jessica said. She reached behind a couch pillow and pulled out a small roll of black tape.

"That doesn't prove anything," Steven said nervously. "And where'd you find that, anyway?"

"In your room. I vacuumed it today. Wasn't that thoughtful of me?"

Steven's brow wrinkled. "I hope you didn't go snooping around my room—"

"Why?" Jessica asked. "Because I might find *this*?" She reached behind the pillow again and pulled out a small book. "Exhibit A," she said. *"Chess for Idiots."*

"So?" Steven said. "I told you I had to learn the rules."

"Then I give you Exhibit B," Jessica said.

"A CD?" Steven said. "What does that prove?"

"Not just any CD. *Wagner's Greatest Hits.* Checked out from the Sweet Valley Public Library."

"So?" Steven repeated. "I was trying to save money. Even geniuses have to budget."

"How about *this*?" Jessica cried. "Volume Twelve of the encyclopedia?"

"That proves I'm not a genius?" Steven demanded.

"Look what page is marked," Jessica said. "The entry on Abraham Lincoln. You underlined the date he was assassinated."

"This is all circumstantial evidence," Steven argued. "You haven't proved your case."

"How about this?" Jessica crowed. She pulled the crumpled answer sheet out of her pocket. "How do you explain why all these Q *and* A answers are written down?"

Steven swallowed. "Would you believe I'm psychic?"

"Come on, Steven," Jessica said triumphantly. "Admit it. You're no more a genius than I am a thief."

Steven sighed. "All right, all right. I admit it. I was trying to play a practical joke on Joe, because I knew he was trying to play a practical joke on me."

"Huh?"

"Ever since I won that basketball bet, he's been talking about getting even. And you know Joe. He's the world's greatest practical joker—next to me, that is. As soon as he suggested we take those IQ tests, I had a feeling he was up to something, but I played along. Then, when I saw the phony letters from MEGA, I was sure. I mean, I *am* brilliant and all—"

"Excuse me while I gag," Jessica interrupted.

"But not *that* brilliant," Steven finished. "Joe made up those letters on his dad's computer. He was probably planning to give me a hard time when I didn't *act* like a genius, or get better grades in school or something."

Jessica laughed.

"But I fooled him when I actually started to act the part. As a matter of fact, I've been driving him crazy. I'm sure he's about ready to confess to the joke."

"But why did you have to involve Elizabeth and me?"

"I figured I'd give you two a hard time, too, since you seemed to think it was so impossible that your big brother could have aced the test. But to tell you the truth, I was getting pretty tired of faking it. I spent half my nights reading the dictionary."

"Poor Joe," Jessica said, laughing. "He was really losing it when you made him watch the porcupine special. You are going to tell him the truth, aren't you?"

Steven shrugged. "I guess it's time. I just have to find the right way."

"Well, you almost had me fooled," Jessica admitted. "But not quite. I know you too well."

"What do you mean by that?"

"The dear sibling thing, Steven. You might call me your sibling, but *dear*? Never."

"I see what you mean." Steven grinned.

"And Steven?"

"What?"

"Remember how I promised I wasn't going to tease you anymore if it turned out you really were a genius?"

"I remember."

"Well, starting right now, you're fair game again, dear sibling."

"Elizabeth, you were so awesome today," Jessica said. The two girls were sitting in the kitchen, eating the cookies Mrs. Wakefield had made.

"Thanks, Jess," Elizabeth said. "I have to admit, I am kind of proud that my snooping skills paid off so well."

"Actually, so did mine," Jessica said with a

grin. "I've been doing a little mystery-solving of my own this afternoon. And I'm afraid I have some devastating news, Lizzie."

"What?" Elizabeth demanded.

"It turns out our big brother isn't a genius, after all. Unless you count being a genius at practical jokes."

"You're sure?"

"Positive. He's just plain old Steven. Trust me."

Elizabeth laughed. "I have to admit I had some doubts about those test results. But I've been sort of preoccupied with the Swiper mystery, and Steven seemed so excited about being a genius that I didn't want to ask too many questions and burst his bubble."

Just then Steven appeared in the doorway. "I just got off the phone with Joe," he announced. "He's coming over here this afternoon, and I'm going to tell him the truth."

"Can we watch?" Jessica asked eagerly.

"You can even help, dear siblings," Steven replied with a devilish grin.

Ten

◇

The twins had just finished up the last of the chocolate-chip cookies when they heard a knock at the door. "I wonder who that is?" Jessica said, running to answer it. "Joe couldn't have gotten here already."

When she opened the door, she saw Lila, Mandy, Ellen, Kimberly, and Janet standing on the front porch. Lila was carrying a big silver helium balloon that had the words "I'm sorry" printed on it. "Here, Jessica," Lila said, passing her the balloon. "This is to apologize for thinking you were a thief."

"Actually, we're *all* sorry, Jessica," Mandy said.

"Can we come in?" Ellen asked.

Jessica pretended to hesitate. After all, there was no point in letting her friends off too easily. "I just don't know," she said with a dramatic sigh, "if things can ever be the same between us. The way you all doubted me . . . you can't imagine the pain it caused." She closed her eyes and pretended to wipe away a tear.

"You can understand why we thought what we did," Janet said. "Veronica's plot was awfully convincing."

"Come on, Jessica," Ellen urged. "It all worked out OK in the end."

Jessica sighed again.

"We've got tons of great gossip to tell you," Lila said.

Jessica grinned. "Well, I *guess* I can probably find it in my heart to forgive you," she said. "But it may take time."

"Not too much time, I hope," Kimberly said. "We brought double-chocolate-chip ice cream, and it's melting."

"Too bad Jessica and I just ate a whole plate of chocolate-chip cookies," Elizabeth said as she joined Jessica at the door.

Jessica shrugged. "I've always got room for ice cream."

The girls headed into the kitchen and gathered around the table. Elizabeth got out bowls and spoons, and Jessica began scooping out the ice cream.

"I have to tell you, it's nice not being a criminal anymore," she said, licking her fingers.

"There's one thing I still don't get," Mandy said. "How did Veronica get hold of your locker combination?"

"Elizabeth and I finally figured that out," Jessica said. "A while ago I lent Veronica my math book. I'd written my combination on the inside cover, just in case I forgot it. That's where she must have gotten it."

"That girl sure is a sneak," Janet said as Jessica handed her a bowl of ice cream.

"She won't be anymore," Lila said.

"What do you mean?" Elizabeth asked.

Lila grinned. "After school, I stopped by the principal's office to drop off a note from my dad excusing me from school tomorrow for a dentist appointment." She made a face, then took a big spoonful of ice cream. "Anyway, I heard Mrs. Knight talking to Mr. Clark, and it turns out Veronica's actually been suspended!"

"Serves her right," Jessica muttered. "Although school's going to be awfully dull without her around, causing trouble."

"Veronica *was* good at that," Lila agreed. "Between the stuff she did at the school dance, and all the stealing . . ." She shook her head guiltily. "I still can't believe I doubted you, Jessica."

"Some people stood by me," Jessica said, casting Elizabeth a grateful smile. "Elizabeth, Amy, Belinda, Aaron—"

"I know another guy who stood by you," Ellen said, grinning.

"Who?" Jessica asked.

"Rick Hunter. I heard him in the hall this afternoon, saying he knew you were innocent."

Jessica frowned. "Are we talking about the same Rick Hunter who teases me every chance he gets?"

"Well," Ellen said sheepishly, "I sort of left out the part where he said you were way too klutzy to be the Swiper."

Jessica rolled her eyes while everyone else laughed. "So what else did I miss today?"

"Oh," Lila exclaimed. "I almost forgot to tell you about the marriage unit!"

"It's this all-school project we'll be doing for two weeks," Mandy explained. "Mr. Seigel said we're going to be learning what it's really like to be married."

"How are we going to do that?" Jessica asked.

"Search me," Janet said. "All I know is, I'd rather study marriage than math."

"Me, too," Jessica said excitedly. "Of course, I'd rather study *anything* than math."

After finishing their ice cream, the girls went into the family room to watch TV.

"Mind if I join you, dear siblings?" Steven asked, sauntering in.

"Dear siblings?" Janet repeated. "I wish you could teach Joe to be that polite, Steven."

"Steven, I thought you were—" Elizabeth began, but Jessica shot her a warning look.

"He's been this way ever since he found out he was a genius," Jessica explained to Janet.

"Joe *could* use some guidance in his comportment," Steven said politely. "Maybe I can help him. As a matter of fact, he's coming over. He should be here any minute."

Janet stood up and motioned for Jessica to join her in the kitchen. "Jessica," she whispered when they were safely out of earshot, "I know this may come as a big shock to you, but this whole genius thing is a practical joke that Joe made up."

Jessica put her hand to her mouth and gasped, pretending to be surprised. "You're kidding! Steven is going to be devastated when he finds out."

"I would have let you in on it sooner, but, well . . . we weren't exactly speaking."

"Poor Steven," Jessica said. "This time Joe really got carried away, Janet."

"What can I say? You know how Joe is."

"Well, *I'm* not going to tell Steven the truth," Jessica said. "It'd break his heart."

"I think Joe's getting ready to, anyway," Janet whispered. "He said the whole joke was getting out of hand. Steven actually made him watch some TV show about porcupines on Friday night!"

Suddenly they heard the doorbell, and then Steven's voice in the front hallway. "I'll bet that's Joe now," Jessica said. "Come on."

"Ah, Jessica," Steven exclaimed, as Jessica and Janet joined everyone in the family room. "I'm glad you're back. There's something I want to announce."

"There's something I want to say, too," Joe said.

"In good time, my friend. This is too important to wait." Steven stood in the middle of the family room, while Joe eyed him nervously. "As you know, I've recently had a revelation about my intellectual status that has virtually transformed my life."

"Steven—" Joe interrupted, but Steven shook his head.

"No longer am I tethered to the tedious concerns of the average sophomore. I've discovered there's a whole wide world out there, waiting for me to explore it; a world of torts and opera and porcupines!"

"Steven," Joe hissed. "I think maybe you and I should talk—privately."

"Do something," Janet whispered to Jessica. "Before Steven totally humiliates himself."

"The things that used to interest me," Steven continued, "horsing around with the guys, going to horror movies, playing basketball—they all seem so, well, *silly* now. That's why I've decided, after much deliberation, to quit school."

"What?" Joe cried, his face frozen in panic.

"Oh, no," Janet muttered.

Elizabeth and Jessica exchanged a secret smile. "I think it's for the best," Elizabeth said. "Maybe you can apply for early admission to Harvard, Steven."

"A brilliant idea, Elizabeth," Steven exclaimed. "I wonder if they accept fourteen-year-olds?" He paced back and forth, his eyes glowing. "I can see me now—a lawyer by the time I'm seventeen! Maybe Dad and I could even work together."

"Jessica, *say* something," Janet urged.

"Steven," Joe said, reaching into his pocket. "There's something I've got to show you." He pulled out a folded piece of paper and handed it to Steven. "I'm sorry, really I am."

There was silence in the room as everyone watched Steven unfold the letter. "But . . . what is it?" Steven murmured.

"It's from the MEGA people," Joe explained softly. "I guess they sent it to me because I put my return address on the test envelopes." He patted Steven on the back. "Tough break, guy."

Steven gazed at the paper, his eyes wide. "But this is impossible!" he cried, clutching the letter to his heart dramatically.

"Steven, what does it say?" Elizabeth asked.

"It says the computer mixed up the results. It says I'm not really a genius," Steven moaned, sinking into a chair.

"But how could they have made such a mistake?" Mandy asked.

"They mixed up the names," Joe explained quickly. "Somewhere out there is a guy named Steven *Woke*field who thinks he only scored above average, when *he's* actually the genius."

"Steven *Woke*field?" Jessica repeated, barely suppressing a smile.

"Anyway, what's wrong with being above average?" Ellen demanded.

"Nothing," Steven moaned. "It's just that I had my heart set on being a genius." Suddenly he grew angry. "There's got to be some kind of mistake," he cried. "How do you explain how smart I've been the past few days, Joe?"

Joe shrugged. "Search me."

"How do you explain the chess, and the Wagner?" Steven cried.

"Yeah," Elizabeth shouted. "And the porcupines?"

Steven turned suddenly and waved the letter in Joe's face. "And while we're at it," he demanded, "how do you explain the fact that whoever wrote this letter misspelled three words?"

Joe's eyes went wide. "I—I'm sure it's just a

clerical error," he stammered, but by then Steven and Jessica and Elizabeth had all dissolved into helpless laughter.

"Give it up, Joe," Steven crowed. "I may not be a genius, but I *can* spell. I know this is a phony letter."

Joe frowned. "You do?"

"I've known all along. I mean, come on! Three hours of porcupines? Don't you know me better than that?"

Joe put his hands on his hips. "You mean the whole time you've been faking this genius stuff?"

"It takes a practical joker to know a practical joker," Steven said, still laughing.

Joe threw up his hands and grinned. "All right, I admit it. You were gloating so much after that basketball contest that I wanted to teach you a lesson. I thought about making myself the genius, but I knew you'd never buy that. Then, when you started to get so carried away, I set this letter up on my dad's computer, just like I did with the first one. I figured it was time to put an end to the whole thing."

"Well, one good thing came out of all this," Steven said. "I'm learning to play chess." He nodded toward the stairway. "Come on. I'll teach you."

"Wouldn't you rather just play yourself?" Joe joked.

"Naw." Steven shook his head. "You're more fun to beat!"

"At least that's over with," Jessica said with a sigh of relief as she watched the boys head upstairs.

Janet shook her head. "Our brothers really are weird sometimes."

"Yeah," Ellen said in a dreamy voice, "but they're awfully cute."

"Not if you're related to them," Elizabeth said with a laugh.

Jessica reached for the remote control. "So what do you want to watch?"

Mandy grinned. "You don't still have that porcupine special on tape, do you?"

"Guess what I found while I was vacuuming today?" Jessica asked, poking her head into Elizabeth's bedroom later that evening.

"If it was under your bed, I probably don't want to know," Elizabeth said, looking up from the book she was reading.

"Actually, they were under *your* dresser." Jessica held out Elizabeth's missing sweater and sweatshirt. "Ta-daaa!"

"My clothes," Elizabeth exclaimed in amazement. "The ones you stole!"

Jessica winced. "I believe you mean *borrowed*," she corrected. "Mom said she found them in the dirty clothes hamper and washed them. She put them on top of your dresser, and I guess they must have fallen down behind it."

"I'm really sorry, Jess," Elizabeth said contritely. "It never even occurred to me to look there."

"That's OK, Lizzie. I know a way you can make it up to me." Jessica gave her twin a big smile. "Can I borrow your white jeans tomorrow?"

Elizabeth laughed. "Yes, you can *borrow* them."

"So what are you reading?" Jessica asked, heading toward Elizabeth's bureau.

"Mrs. Arnette assigned us a chapter to read for the marriage unit."

"But that's not starting until next week."

"I know. But it's really kind of interesting. There's a lot more hard work that goes into being married than you realize."

"Work?" Jessica repeated. "Being married isn't work, it's fun. Just imagine how romantic it is. When I think of marriage, I think of Jake and Shelby setting up house in Hollywood, having their glamorous friends over for parties. And Shelby will always wear beautiful designer clothes—"

"Yeah, right," Elizabeth said skeptically. "And Jake will wear tuxedos while he takes out the garbage."

Jessica laughed. "Exactly."

"I don't know, Jessica. I get the feeling Mr. Seigel has something different in mind."

Just how romantic is the marriage project going to be? Find out in Sweet Valley Twins and Friends #68, **THE MIDDLE SCHOOL GETS MARRIED.**